The Lion in the Room Next Door

"Spellbinding. . . . One to be read and re-read with aston-
ished appreciation."   – *London Free Press*

"Merilyn Simonds is an accomplished alchemist. . . ."
                                        – *National Post*

"These aren't just the stories of one life; here are the patterns
found in all our lives, richly celebrated."
                                – Gail Anderson-Dargatz

"An accomplished, at times exhilarating collection."
                                        – *Eye* magazine

"Unflichingly observed, intensely realized, and beautifully
evoked."   – Ronald Wright

"What is remarkable about these stories is the intensity of
feeling in the writing and its sheer quality. The observation
of the details of life are Chekhovian in their accuracy. . . ."
                                – *Publishing News* (U.K.)

"Haunting. . . . The stories are seductive, melancholy and
dark, sensual and sexual. Danger, assault, or loss is revealed,
sometimes unexpectedly, or lurking just around the corner,
just under the surface."   – *Booklist* (starred review) (U.S.)

"Wise, potent, and luminous. . . . This book is an event, a revelation of the fact that, for better or worse, everything
matters."   – Diane Schoemperlen

THE LION IN THE
ROOM NEXT DOOR

⌣

M E R I L Y N   S I M O N D S

Canadian Cataloguing in Publication Data

Simonds, Merilyn, 1949-
The lion in the room next door

ISBN 0-7710-8066-2 (bound) ISBN 0-7710-8067-0 (pbk.)

1. Simonds, Merilyn, 1949- . I. Title.

PS8587.I46Z53 1999   C818'.5403   C98-933031-1
PR9199.3.S5194Z47 1999

We acknowledge the financial support of the Government of
Canada through the Book Publishing Industry Development
Program for our publishing activities. We further acknowledge the
support of the Canada Council for the Arts and Ontario Arts
Council for our publishing program.

Cover design and photo manipulation: Sari Ginsberg
Cover photographs: Martyn Rose / Photonica (top)
Yvonne Catterson / Photonica (bottom)

Set in Bembo by M&S, Toronto
Printed and bound in Canada

McClelland & Stewart Inc.
The Canadian Publishers
481 University Avenue
Toronto, Ontario
M5G 2E9

1 2 3 4 5   04 03 02 01 00

For my sisters

For navigators who love the wind, memory is a port of departure.

– EDUARDO GALEANO
  Walking Words

Memory believes before knowing remembers.

– WILLIAM FAULKNER
  Light in August

CONTENTS

SAUDADES (Yearnings)

The Lion in the Room Next Door   3
King of the Cowboys, Queen of the West   17
Nossa Senhora dos Remédios   35
The Blue of the *Madrugada*   53

LIPES (Sorrows)

Navigating the Kattegat   87
The Distance to Delphi   117
Taken for Delirium   145
The Still Point   165

MILAGROS (Miracles)

In the City of the Split Sky   183
Song of the Japanese White-Eye   209
The Day of the Dead   229

Acknowledgements   257

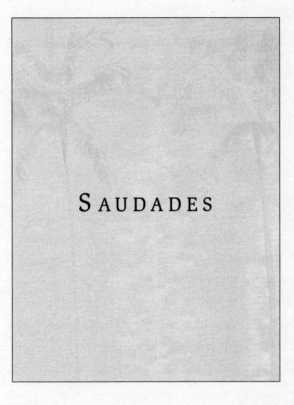

SAUDADES

THE LION IN THE ROOM NEXT DOOR

I remember only the end. I don't know when it began: the low rumble like an earthquake's first tremor, felt through the soles of the feet. No one heard it but me.

I lie in my bed in the darkened hotel room, so far away from home, and listen to this sound of the night. Closer it rolls, then away, like thunder or the changes in our lives. My three sisters in their beds next to mine are asleep; in this room and in the hall outside, silence. Then the rumble moves through the wall by my head and I lie very still between the sheets. I think: When it comes too close, I will wake my mother and father who sleep in the room next to ours, on the other side. But the tremor recedes like the tide, my fear ebbs too, and I sleep.

Because I always woke early, I became expert at slipping unnoticed from sleeping rooms.

I pinch the lock and ease it one degree at a time toward the vertical, holding it back at the very last second so as to dull the heavy sound of the bolt as it settles into its slot in the door. This morning, I execute the first phase perfectly. The lock retracts as smoothly and silently as a turtle drawing in its head. I grasp the doorknob in my fists and turn it ever so slowly, leaning into the work until the latch is fully retracted. Then, pressing against the wood to guard against my own eagerness, I pull open the door, holding my breath and listening for the first cry of the hinge that might give me away.

A sister turns in her sleep. I stop. She flings her arm out from the bedclothes. Under cover of the rustling sheets, I take my chance and widen the gap the rest of the way.

Slipping into the hall, I reverse my pantomime, twisting the knob, pulling the door to, easing the latch soundlessly into the frame.

I pause for several minutes. No one stirs. The row of doors that open onto the third-floor hallway, like eyelids, stay tightly closed. The indigo carpet beckons beneath my feet.

I learned how to spy in those silent golden dawns. I made the Hotel Terminus my own.

Quietly I pad along its halls, taking the stairs from floor to floor. Now and then, I see a maid. I smile when she says, —*Bom dia, senhorinha,* catching her words between my lips and when she is gone, rolling them on my tongue, foreign yet familiar; oddly, faintly sweet, like the dew from an exotic fruit.

Fearless in my solitude, I listen outside strangers' doors. Mostly, I prowl near Room 32, the room next to ours that rumbles through the hot, still nights. But all I hear is my own breath, short and quick, in my ear.

My father ate his breakfast alone, or perhaps not at all.

I sit in the corner of the lobby, hidden by the half-grown palms, watching as he emerges from behind the elevator's filigreed brass gate, tall and handsome with his pencil-line moustache and tightly curling hair. He walks with purpose past the man at the desk, nods and says words in Portuguese as if he has been speaking this language all his life. At the door, silhouetted in the light, he takes a cigarette from the package in his chest pocket. He leans to light it and tosses the match into the brass cylinder of fine white sand pressed with the hotel crest. The door closes behind him, but I can still see him through the palm leaves, through the glass, standing on the wildly patterned sidewalk. His Arrow shirt lies white, dry, and crisp against his brown arms. His skin is dark as a Brazilian's, burnt coffee-red by summer sun; ours, my sisters', my mother's, my own, still pale as cream. He stands and waits for his driver, smoking his cigarette, glancing sometimes at his watch, sometimes down the street, shifting his weight from one foot to the other. He looks impatient, I think, grinding his half-smoked cigarette under the polished toe of his shoe. Then he is gone, and the black and white paving stones swirl to the curb, empty and free.

To pass the days, my mother, my sisters, and I rode the *bondes*, open streetcars where passengers would sit on benches, exposed, or hang precariously off railings at either side.

We take a different streetcar each day, travelling through cobbled streets, past dusty rows of squared-off stucco houses that bump up against the sidewalks, no arm's length of grass to keep some distance. Here, doors open directly onto pavement or hover behind walls crusted on top with broken glass, though occasionally I see a shock of brilliant yellow or tangerine foliage rising to escape over the barricades.

My two older sisters sit on one bench; my mother, the baby, and I, behind. Me, on the outside of the open car, where the breeze ruffles my dark curls; the baby, on my mother's knee, a blonde and blue-eyed talisman that draws old women and young men to my mother's side, mouthing words, waving their hands, wanting, I think, to touch her, to touch me.

Late in the day, we walk to the park in front of the apartment building where we will live one day soon. We sit in the dusk and listen to the brass band play marching songs. Only the old men and women and the very young children sit and listen. The others walk slowly around the bandstand, a human merry-go-round, the women walking in a circle on the inside, the men on the outside walking in the opposite direction so that they move toward each other, never stopping. It seems strange to me, this endless circling that is almost a dance, like the do-si-do of the Saturday-night square dances in the town hall back home, except that here, even in the breaks between songs, the men and women keep on walking, exchanging brief words as they pass, the moving file of women enclosed forever between the bandstand and the circling men.

My older sisters join the young women walking. My mother plays with the baby near the poinsettia bushes where we once saw a pair of cardinals, not solidly red like the ones in Canada but white and grey with scarlet heads like woodpeckers and with beaks that glinted silver in the sun.

I keep my distance from the bandstand, sit alone under the royal palms that edge the square, lean my head back against the bench, and watch the fronds waving far, far above, dark wings against an amber sky.

Once, when the others left on some excursion, though I was only eight years old, I stayed behind, I don't know why.

I sit on the cool marble of the third-floor landing, propped against the wall. From here, I can see both the brass door of the elevator cage and the long blue hallway. I wait. Wait for the door of Room 32 to open. Wait for the mystery of the rhythms in the night to be revealed.

I believe that with perfect concentration I can make the elevator stop at my floor, and sometimes it does. The gate folds back, and a serious, suited man strides past me, past Room 32. Later, when the gate folds back again, the plump pink Americans who live in the suite at the end of the hall look at me oddly. The hotel is full of Americans. My mother says they too are waiting for their houses to be ready. Like my father, the men are here to start factories. But we are the only Canadians, and these Americans, though they seem to speak our language, are foreign to me: their accents are peculiar, their manners too bold. When they greet me I nod, but I don't say a word.

The maids pass behind me, up and down the stairs. The air grows sweet and moist with chocolate.

When a man in a floppy white hat stops at the landing and, smiling, invites me up the stairs, I climb after him into the fragrant, thickening haze. We pass through a locked door that opens to the hotel's top floor. I think: Perhaps it lives here, whatever it is that rumbles through the night. Perhaps my ears have tricked me and the sound comes from above, not from the room next to mine.

The man leads me into a kitchen where long tables are laid with candies and desserts, cream-filled tarts topped with sliced mangoes and strawberries arranged in patterns and sealed in glaze, chocolate eclairs and pastries thick as cake but flaky like pie crust, shattering into crumbs at the first bite. The same sweets line the glass-fronted cabinet in the coffee shop beside the hotel lobby where, on Saturdays, my father buys me grilled ham-and-cheese sandwiches and *guaraná* while he drinks *cuba libres* with a slice of lime.

The man in the white hat sweeps his arm over the trays. Have whatever you like, the gesture seems to say. His words sound coaxing. I can't think why it would be forbidden, but

I know I am right to refuse. I shake my head, all the while scanning the ovens, the churning machines fitted with nozzles and rotating bowls. But the sound is not the same. What I hear in the night is not gears and whirring metal. It not only moves, it breathes.

In the evening, when my father returned to the hotel, his white shirt would be limp, stained red at the collar.

I think it is blood. Dust from the road, he says. Paler dust collects in the creases of his skin, under his eyes, and in the scallops of thickened flesh at his elbows. That is how I know he is old: the way his skin gathers at the joints, dry and darkened with so much bending.

This is a time to be quiet, now, to walk the baby up and down the hall, to sit on the leather couches in the lobby with my sisters, our hair neatly combed, our dresses freshly ironed, mine the colour of limes with a black velvet ribbon threaded through eyelet lace across my chest. Four girls, their mother and father upstairs.

When we walk at last into the dining room, the man at the piano changes his tune. "Que Sera, Sera" he plays as we make our entrance. His nods and smiles are so elaborate that everyone in the room turns to watch us take our place at the table by the window.

The waiter in his white coat turns aside the linen cloth he carries and, with silver tongs, lays a hard roll on each side plate. We sit up very straight and watch my father sprinkle his pat of butter with salt, mashing the two together with his fork, then spreading it thickly on the soft, warm centre of the bread. He picks up an olive, sucks off the flesh, and adds the brown pit flecked with green to the others lined up on the white tablecloth.

Chicken fried with plantain and, after that, *creme de caramelo*. We do not speak while we eat. The piano player plays. When we rise to leave, the man slides again to our song. "Whatever Will Be, Will Be. Que Sera, Sera."

And in the night, in the endless summer night, while my sisters sleep, I lie still and small in my bed and wait for the rhythm from the other side of the wall to begin. Over. And over. And over again. Then, other sounds too. A low, gentle urging, I think.

I collect them like shells washed up on a beach: the tremor, the heave and roll, back and forth, back and forth. We have lived in the hotel for so long now, I am lulled by the motion to sleep.

One morning, as I eased my door silently closed, the door beside it moved.

I cannot look, I have yet to slip the latch into the frame, but I can hear, above my own breath, the other one clicking shut, footsteps drawing near. And something else, too.

As I turn, a man passes. Beside him walks a lion. Her fur is smooth, the colour of deserts or sun-scorched plains.

Though her paws against the carpet make no sound, I feel each tread, a tingling through the soles of my shoes. Her eyes, when she looks at me, are soft with secrets.

— *Bom dia, senhorita*, says the man who holds the leash.

— *Bom dia*, I hear myself reply, as if I have spoken these words all my life.

He presses the button for the elevator. The lion swings her tail and bends her neck to gaze back at me standing fixed by my own closed door. Then the brass gate folds open, and the man and the lion disappear. I stand alone in the long blue hall. A faint scent of feline. A memory of topaz eyes.

At the Hotel Terminus, breakfast was never served in the main dining room. We ate instead on the second floor, in a smaller, brighter place: a long gallery with wicker tables and floor-to-ceiling windows that opened onto balconies hardly wide enough to stand on.

This morning my mother and I, for some reason, are alone. I have her all to myself, such a rare occurrence that the little bones in the vicinity of my heart quiver as they do on Christmas morning, or on my birthday, or when I am certain something wonderful is about to happen. We sit in a shaft of lemon sunlight. On our table is a basket of hard rolls, a dish of marmalade, a small silver platter of butter and two silver pots with arched spouts, one filled with thick dark chocolate, the other steamed milk.

— There's a lion in the room next door, I say.

I do not look at my mother's face. Instead, I watch the surface of my chocolate thicken, biding my time until she responds. Finally, I lean to the edge of the cup and suck up the jellied skin in one long breath.

—Don't slurp your chocolate, she says.

—The lion . . .

—Don't be silly.

She brushes chips of bread crust off her pressed linen lap.
—There are no lions in hotels, she says.

As she turns to look at me, she grows large. Her hand, reaching out, stretches, a long bleached eel. Her body swells. It presses against the walls. Her hair scrapes against the light. Her head, as she stares at me, wavers, a balloon in languid air. Her lips shape words, but I cannot make them out. I think she says I should not tell stories. But she is too far away to hear.

Still, I believed in what I alone had seen.

In the nights I lie awake listening and in the early hours of the dawn, I wander the hotel hallways, hoping to see the lion again, or the man who held the leash.

Days pass. Then weeks. Until one night, I don't know when, the gentle rhythms stop.

And so I put an end to my early-morning prowls, my vigils behind the palms. I am sad but not broken-hearted, for somehow the lion is made more real by its loss. I know it's gone yet I think I hear the lion, still rolling through the night, and, for reasons I don't quite understand, I take comfort from the sound.

One day, shortly before we moved out of the Hotel Terminus, the American girl from the suite at the end of the hall invited me to play. My mother agreed. It would be good for me, she said.

The American girl has cut-out dolls to dress, cardboard girls with pouting smiles, their party dresses and beach costumes fitted with well-placed tabs, gaily wrapped gifts and sand pails with slits that slide neatly over the outstretched fingers of their hands. We spend all day together, and that night, too.

A sleepover. Our parents are playing bridge down the hall, close enough that through the open door we can hear low outbursts of men's laughter, our mothers' voices like trilling birds. We are sitting on the bed, playing in our nighties, when the boy from across the hall walks in. He is a big boy, like the ones in the schoolyard back home who would grab the back of my swing, their hands close by my bum, and, pushing me up high, would run underneath, twisting the swing as they let go, making it careen crazily, crashing into the swings on either side, me hanging on for dear life, too terrified to utter a sound.

The boy picks up the cut-out dolls spread between us on the bed and pulls off the pails and presents, then the perky straw hats and gloves, the bolero and the red flared skirt, the swimsuit, the lace evening gown. He plucks off their clothing one piece at a time, a slow striptease, tearing the carefully folded tabs, laughing as the flimsy paper wardrobe flutters to the floor.

The American girl giggles. He is her friend. I've watched them play together, dangerous games, running from one end of the hall to the other, knocking on every door, then crouching behind the maid's trolley as, one by one, the doors were flung open and stern-faced men and women peered out of their rooms, eyeing me suspiciously as I sat on the floor by the elevator, waiting.

She joins in the boy's game now too, wrenching the doll from my hands and ripping off its clothes, flinging them from the bed, dress and slip and shoes pirouetting to the floor. They watch the last paper doll fall, naked except for white panties, painted on. As they lean together, laughing, I slip off the bed to the floor, trying to distance myself from them, aware of my own nakedness under the flimsy pink nylon of my nightie.

But the boy has spotted me. He is on his hands and knees, creeping across the floor. I feel the roughness of the carpet on my bum as I squirm back against the wall. I don't know what he intends to do, but something about the way he stares at me makes me draw my knees up close, press my arms against the floor to hold down my nightgown, sealing off the triangle made by my bent legs.

He stops in front of me. I stifle the sound at the back of my throat, force myself to be perfectly still. Maybe this, too, is just one of their games.

He touches my feet, takes the hem of my nightie in his fists. The girl on the bed giggles again.

—Should I? he says to her, though he never takes his eyes off me. —Yeah, I think I should.

My hands tighten against the nylon, holding it to my sides, but I am no match for him. He lifts his arms, and my nightie too, shoves his head underneath, the pink fabric a tent and him inside, his hands between my knees now, pulling them apart, looking, looking at me, looking at me naked in that place between my legs.

I turn my head away. And then I see her, there in the open doorway, her tawny fur drifting like dunes. She lowers her haunches and I am beside her, sliding onto her back, my legs spread barely wide enough. My nightie (what luck!) is torn in exactly the right place. It drapes across her flanks, reaches down to cover my feet. I glide my hands along her neck, feel her pulse in my palms. Slowly she rises and, our eyes straight ahead, we set off down the hall, swaying with silent footsteps, and vanish into the night.

KING OF THE COWBOYS, QUEEN OF THE WEST

—∿—

Hanging by my throat, my shirt blotting red, I thought: My father means to kill the horse. Then: No, he means to make my sister kill it.

At the first gunshot I'd run from the road toward my family gathered in the field in front of the *fazenda*. I didn't see the wire fence. It hit me in the chest, my feet slid out from under me, and I was impaled on the barb that caught in the soft flesh of my neck under my chin.

The distant scene played itself out in silence. There was the family. The horse. And the gun. In my recollection, they are connected, the family assembled to shoot the horse, which can't be true, even though Honey was a sad old swayback, a sour-breathed mare that gratefully gobbled the sugar cubes I'd sneak from the table.

I've always contrived to keep out of my family's way, which was why I was down at the road in the first place,

poking at the plants that shrivelled in the sun, while everyone else lounged in the cowhide-and-bentwood chairs on
the verandah or swayed in string hammocks, stirring the air
as they moved back and forth, cooling their toes on the terracotta tiles.

The *fazenda* wasn't ours. It belonged to a European
couple, friends of my parents who invited us during the dry
season to escape the scalding city streets. They lived just
outside Vinhedo, the village where my father's factory was,
in a long, low house slung across the crest of a barren hill.
The rooms inside were dark and cool as caves. All the surfaces, the chairs and tables of mimosa wood, were smooth,
no decorative carving or fancy cloths to catch and hold the
heat. Every morning, the maid would pull the shutters to
and they'd stay closed until sunset, although after the mid-
day meal she would open the slatted doors to the verandah
and allow the pent-up gloom to spill out. That was where
we'd take our siesta. But I was nine years old, I saw no reason
to rest.

– Can't you sit still for five minutes? my mother had
moaned after lunch that day.

I'd stood by the back of her chair, my lips close to her ear,
compelled by the heaviness of the air to keep my voice low
as I asked permission to leave. I was about to open my mouth
again, to explain how I was afraid I'd suffocate in the shadowed heat, or metamorphose into a scaly-skinned gecko like
the ones that watched us, bug-eyed, from the walls. How I
couldn't bear the thin line of my father's moustache, or my

baby sister's precious gurgling, or the green taste of the mashed-guava dessert that clotted at the back of my throat. But just in time I remembered what I'd been learning, that it was best to keep such things to myself.

—Oh, go on then, she'd sighed, waving me away with her palm-leaf fan. —But don't wander too far.

The light, when I stepped off the verandah, slapped my eyes shut. I bent my head against the sun and walked away from the house, exulting in my deliverance. The trees, the bushes, the grass, even the adobe walls of the *fazenda* glowed as if God himself had gilded the landscape. Only the road showed a different hue, a dusty garnet, which my father had told me came from iron in the soil but which I believed was the red dye that lured Portuguese sailors through the Doldrums to the shores of Brazil.

I walked down the red road, away from the fields, toward the wilderness, a *bandeirante*, an expedition of one, in search not of dye or diamonds or tattooed slaves with animal horns fitted over their private parts, but of anything, really, nothing I could name. The bushes on either side rustled with life, buzzed with a thin, high-pitched siren call I could not resist. I poked in the grasses, parting them with a stick for fear my fingers might touch the skin of a snake or a fire ant by mistake. I was cautious with good cause. I had once seen a boa, wider around than the thickest part of my leg, coiled in a tree above the path. Hairy white spiders, their bodies big as saucers, always lurked among the empty *guaraná* bottles by the maids' quarters. And just that morning, the sister next oldest to me had been ordered to stand perfectly still while my father took the cigarette from his mouth and pressed it against the shiny black body of the tick that burrowed its head into the skin of her arm.

Still, I was drawn to the road's wild edge. I waded into the grasses as if they were the sea, uncertain of my footing but continuing nonetheless, heading for the bamboo thatch that would close over my head.

It was the sound of the gun that stopped me. I ran toward my family, straight into the barbed-wire fence.

They had moved off the verandah and were gathered in the field, my sisters' pale cotton dresses and my father's white shirt wavering in the veil of heat between us. I could not call out. If I moved, the barb would tear deeper into my throat.

No one looked my way. They were turned toward my oldest sister. Her arm was extended and her head was tilted so it almost touched her shoulder. My father stood tight against her back, his arm reaching alongside hers, his cheek resting on her head, the two of them cradled together like nesting dolls. The horse nosed quizzically toward their out-stretched arms.

The sun caught the barrel of the gun and the glint flashed in my eye, fixing the scene like an old-fashioned photograph that blackened at the edges as I swooned.

I barely heard the second shot, I never saw the tin can spiralling through the air, but as darkness enveloped me, I thanked the angels, for the horse still stood, unharmed.

The scar above my Adam's apple is barely perceptible, a small, raised tautness of skin. I worry it with my finger as I contemplate the gun, innocent as a hairbrush, lying in the bottom drawer of my father's bedside table. It is small, smaller than the gun I had seen aimed at the horse all those years ago, though it is not the size but the heft of it as I lift it out of the drawer that makes me recoil into myself.

The smell of the harbour at Santos washes over me. I was almost ten years old. We had just returned to Brazil from a two-month visit home to Canada and, although our ship was docked, the air was still thick with salt and heat and engine oil, the scent of voyage. I was gathering my things together, my comic books, my playing cards, my cut-out dolls, when my mother knocked on the door.

—Your father wants to see you, she said to me. —Wear your coat.

I stood before him, solemn, trying not to show how pleased I was to be so honoured, the only daughter in the room. He was a tall man, but he was sitting, and the peculiar perspective, seeing him eye to eye, threw me off guard, so much so I didn't notice at first that several guns lay strewn on the bed. My father pulled me to him and with one hand opened the right side of my coat. With the other hand he reached for a gun.

The coat was new: red twill the colour of poinsettias on one side, grey lamb's-wool on the other. My mother had bought it for me in New Orleans, where we'd boarded the ship. For hours we'd wandered the cobbled streets under wedding-cake railings, trying on one coat after another. My father, not usually part of our shopping expeditions, insisted on a reversible. My mother agreed. Stout enough to stand up to tropical downpours, she told the clerks, and warm enough for winters in Brazil, which we'd once scorned but which chilled us now, too. It could hardly have been the case but that coat stands in my memory as the first piece of clothing I wore that did not bear the shape of my older sisters.

The coat was too hot, the wool itchy against my skin. My father pushed the gun into the inside pocket and held me away from him. One side of the coat drooped heavily.

– Give her another one, why don't you?

The voice came from behind me. Startled, I swung around to look, the gun hitting my knee. A man was leaning against the porthole. He must have been there all along, partly hidden by the high-backed chairs. I recognized him immediately. It was my father's friend, the American who often appeared at our house unexpectedly and alone, though I knew he had a wife in the back country somewhere to the south. He strolled over to the bed, picked up a gun, and handed it to my father, who slipped it into the pocket on the other side of my coat.

Both men stared at me. The American lit a cigarette, inhaled deeply. He was dressed all in khaki, with knee-high boots of some smooth, supple leather that I wanted to touch, it looked so animal-soft, so rare.

– Why, that's better, he drawled, bending close.

I could smell the treacly dark rum from the *cuba libres* he and my father were drinking.

He poked my belly, making me giggle. – Just like a real cowgirl, huh?

I put one hand in my pocket. Through the fabric that separated the red twill from the lamb's-wool, my fingers found the muzzle. It felt cool to the touch, even under the cloth. Tentatively I felt along the shaft to the chamber that held the bullets, and ever so carefully traced around the thin half-moon of metal, avoiding the trigger that hung inside.

– Okay, let's see you walk, my father said.

The corridor between the bed and the chairs was narrow. Hardly enough room to swing a cat, my father had said when the chief steward showed us our staterooms, and that's what I thought of as I walked unsteadily between my father and his friend: dead cats in burlap sacks knocking against my legs. It made me want to cry but I smiled instead, to show them how easy it was, squaring my hips and spreading my knees against the pull of the guns.

I knew this walk. I'd practised it for hours in my grand-father's backyard in the small Ontario village where we'd lived until I was seven. I wore a gun-belt then, buckled just below my waist, with real leather holsters for my six-shooters, silver with pearl handles. The outfit included a white cowboy hat that had a sliding red clasp to tighten the strings under my chin; a blue denim vest with a plastic fringe that bent every which way no matter how carefully I laid it in my drawer at night; and a skirt with *Dale Evans* spelled out in pale-blue lariat letters along the hem. But it was Roy who was my hero. I wore chinos instead.

Roy was King of the Cowboys, Dale was Queen of the West. While Roy patrolled the range, she stayed back at the Eureka Café, dishing out words of wisdom to the old men and young children who sat at the counter. Watching *The Roy Rogers Show* was a Saturday-morning ritual that I never missed, even in Brazil, where Roy and Dale and Roy's side-kick, Pat, all spoke Portuguese. I'd turn on the little black-and-white television and there was Roy on his palomino, racing down the trail, Dale and Pat galloping behind, never quite catching up. They always helped out, they did as they were told, but it was Roy who gave the orders, Roy who saved the day. The names of their horses said it all. Who would choose a mare called Buttermilk over Trigger, Roy's stallion, fast as a gunshot and twice as true?

Sometimes I rode the sawed-off branch of my grand-father's Spy apple tree, thrilling to the slap of guns at my sides. But mostly I preferred to stalk. Alone, I'd creep up the path to the henhouse, fingers flared above the pearly handles. I'd spin around, draw a bead on the rooster, turn sharply, and draw again, and again, until the guns leapt into my hands slick as anything. Then I'd twirl each one on my trigger finger, and, with a flick of my wrist, nose it back into its holster. I was that good. And I never fired a shot.

I sit down on my parents' bed and settle the gun awkwardly in my lap. It is even heavier than I remember, though I'd been terrified as I'd walked down the ship's gangplank toward the customs officers that the weight of the two guns in my pockets would be enough to drown me if I tripped and fell.

I wonder what happened to the other guns. I've never had the nerve to ask, not since I overheard my father say he'd bought this one in Brazil. For protection against *bandeirantes*, he'd said, telling the story of the diamond-hunting trip he'd made to the interior, hundreds of kilometres from where we lived. The friend who met us on the ship had gone on the expedition too.

He is visiting now, and all afternoon he and my father have been drinking *cuba libres* and reminiscing about Minas Gerais, where the rivers flowing from the jungle are said to glitter with gold and precious gems, where once they'd gone to seek their fortunes, guns strapped to their hips. They are waiting for me in the backyard now, waiting for me to bring the gun.

Bits of their conversation blow through the open window. I resist the urge to lower the pane and draw the curtains, as if to shut out a rising summer storm, the kind of storm I've come to associate with this place. Not a sudden glorious downpour but one that gathers slowly, the sky taking on colour like wounded skin, the thunder muffled at first, then ominous, moving closer, until lightning strafes the clouds, though even then it might blow over, you never knew.

I still have trouble interpreting such signs, although three years have passed since we returned to Canada, to this village we'd left. My father could have stayed in South America, or he could have gone to Australia, or Mexico, or Niagara Falls, but instead he chose to bring us back here, where the familiar seems strange, where even my memories seem out of place; wrong, somehow.

Which is why, although I am fifteen now and practically an adult, I still keep to myself. I avoid my parents' company whenever possible. Today, especially, I want to be alone. When I came home from my job at the grocery store, I didn't think I could bear to be with my father, not after what I'd just seen. But there he was, lounging in the backyard with his friend. They were sitting in the Muskoka chairs under the dying elms, their long legs stretched out, their heads thrown back as they laughed out loud at each other's jokes. Even sitting, they seemed to swagger. I tried to duck into the back door of the house, but my father called to me.

– Hey, look who's here!

The presence of company generally softened the rules. I might have got away with only a wave, but I didn't have the heart, just then, to ignore my father. Reluctantly I crossed the yard to join the men.

– Well, aren't you the young lady! his friend exclaimed.
– Sit down here with us a bit.

I sat on the grass at their feet. Perhaps, I thought, my easy compliance would make them forget about me, so that before too long I could slip away. I listened to their reminiscences, hoping, at least, to be transported to the southern landscape they were conjuring, but my father's Brazil was nothing like the place I'd known.

The exaggerated camaraderie my father indulged in with this man irritated me. Their senseless jokes, their hollow boasts, their inflated opinions of themselves quickly became intolerable. What did they know? Didn't they ever look at the world around them? Blind, self-satisfied old men! I was just about to leave when the conversation took another turn, from gold to guns to how well each could shoot.

—We'll see about that, my father said, then turned to me. —Go get my gun. It's in my bottom drawer, by the bed.

He didn't have to tell me. I already knew. I had discovered it soon after we got back to Canada. I'd just turned twelve and was honing in earnest my skills as a spy. I would wait until the house was empty, inventing reasons to stay alone, and then I'd steal into my older sisters' bedrooms. I would ransack their dressers, fingering their garter belts, holding their brassieres against the swellings on my chest. I searched under their pillows and mattresses, behind the shoe racks in their closets, until I found their diaries, which I jimmied with a bobby pin and read backwards, page by page, careful to check for telltale hairs like the ones I placed so expertly across my own things to alert me to intruders.

When I grew bored with my sisters' secrets, I ventured into my parents' bedroom, investigated their dressers too, touching my father's stiffly ironed shirts, his neatly folded underwear, my mother's silky camisoles and slips, opening one drawer after another as if looking for some concealed evidence, some hidden clue as to who these people really were, until, in the bottom drawer of my father's bedside table, I came across the gun and, on my mother's side, underneath her passport, the small paper packages that held the jewels.

From that day on, whenever I was by myself, all through those first few months back in the country where I'd been born, I'd head straight to my parents' room. I'd lift the gun to my nose, breathe in the sharp, feral smell of Brazil. Then

I'd lay it carefully on the bedspread and go to my mother's bedside table, removing the tiny packages and opening them one by one to reveal aquamarine teardrops, oblongs of amethyst and pink quartz, finely cut ovals of tourmaline, carnelian, and citrine.

The jewels were from Minas Gerais. When my father left on his expedition to the interior, I'd expected him to return with sacks of glittering rock, bullet holes in the van, a blood-soaked bandage wrapped around his head. But he had come back unharmed, not with diamonds or gold but with these semi-precious stones, each one on a square of cotton batting nestled inside a neatly folded strip of paper and labelled, as if he'd bought them in a store.

I loved to spread the jewels on the chenille, scoop them up in my hands, and let them tumble back to the bed, dribbling them through my fingers so they'd catch the light as they fell, tossing rose and amber spangles on the walls. But, always, my pleasure would be stilled by fear. Fear that I might be discovered. I wasn't afraid that I'd be punished, but that my secret forays would have to end. And so I'd put away the gun and scramble to wrap up the jewels, careful to match the stones with the faintly pencilled names, opening the papers and checking, again and again, to make sure each was in its proper place before I returned the little packages to my mother's drawer.

I was never found out. No one noticed me. It was my father who was the centre of attention in our house. A man of few words, even his silence was compelling, although once we knew the rules, he wasn't usually hard to please. Since we'd come back to Canada, though, his mood had changed.

His disapproval was relentless now. We never spoke of this, my mother, my sisters, and I, but as if by some agreement we stayed out of his way. We kept to the periphery where we lay in wait for this new-old place to feel like home again.

There was only one thing that seemed to soothe him: the shiny brochures stacked beside his living-room chair. He'd study them for hours, until finally, last New Year's Eve, he announced abruptly, – I'm going to do it. Right now. I'm not going to miss the Rose Bowl Parade.

It was almost midnight, but still he telephoned the man who owned the village hardware store, and by the time we got up on New Year's Day my father was fussing with the aerial and adjusting the knobs that turned the faces inside the mahogany cabinet of his new colour television first florid, then bilious green. When he'd created flesh tones to his satisfaction, he gathered us in the living room and sat us down behind a line he'd marked on the carpet with the toe of his shoe, ordering us never to sit any closer to the screen.

– Isn't that something? he exclaimed. – Isn't that something? Just look at that colour!

And my sisters and my mother obliged him by going into raptures over the electric-blue roses and the bottle-green chrysanthemums, the Colgate-red lips of the majorettes twirling Ivory-white batons into the grey, pouring rain.

I despised them all. The village, I knew, would already be whispering with this latest proof of our extravagance. The colour television, like the new maroon Buick, like the places we'd been, would only add to whatever it was that separated us from them.

I stood up to leave, my string of excuses ready as my father turned from the television to me.

—Wait, he said. —You'll want to see this.

As if on cue, an invisible band began to play "Happy Trails," and the announcer declared: —Here's Roy Rogers, folks, live and in colour at the Rose Bowl Parade.

Buttermilk and Trigger loomed on the screen, not the real mare and stallion, of course, but oversized reproductions modelled in chicken wire and spray-painted flowers, the flesh-and-blood Dale and Roy propped on top, smiles creased into their cheeks. Roy's face was furrowed with wrinkles. My hero, king of my childhood, when had he grown so old? Rain cascaded off his Stetson, pasting his pale, embroidered shirt to his shrunken chest. A decrepit, pathetic cowboy on a ridiculous fake horse. How could he let himself be made an exhibition of like that? But either he didn't notice or he wasn't letting on that he cared, for he waved jauntily to the crowd, brandishing his six-shooters. Boxed by the television set flickering in my father's living room, the guns looked like toys, harmless and insignificant.

Through the curtains on the bedroom window, I can hear the banter of my father and his American friend, jocular and mocking, and then my father's voice, hollering up to me, —What's taking you so long in there?

I can't delay any longer. I could put the gun away and go to my room, as if homework or fatigue had distracted me from my mission. But, no, I will do this for him.

The gun, when I stand up, suddenly seems unwieldy. I can't think how to carry it. I try holding it muzzle down, dangling it by my side, but the posture seems too careless, too familiar. And so I lay it on the flat of my palm and bear it before me like an offering, through the house, into the kitchen, pushing open the screen door with my hip, following the gun out into the yard.

My father's laugh draws me on, across the grass. There is nothing melodious or joyful about the sound. I hear it as a bark, a howl of pain.

I close my eyes against the memory of what happened this afternoon. But I can no longer refuse what I saw.

A gaping scream, painted on a white bedsheet gathered into a neck and crudely stitched to make arms and legs, the head and body stuffed with straw. The effigy hung by its neck from a pole, a sign scrawled on the chest: BOSS. A crowd had gathered around it, mostly men, strikers with picket signs resting on their shoulders like muskets. They blocked the sidewalk in front of the factory that takes up the centre of the village.

The thought hit me like a hot wind, colouring my cheeks: The straw man is my father. My father, who has worked in the factory since he was young, whose first job, my mother often reminds me, was sweeping floors. He knows these men; they work for him. I know them too. I go to school with their children, sit beside them in church, sell them cigarettes and chocolate bars in the village store.

It was too late to turn back, to take the long way home along the river, cutting through the cow pasture and the woods behind our house. I had to keep walking. I had to pretend I didn't see, or if I saw, that I didn't understand, or if I understood, that it didn't matter, I didn't care.

When I came close, the voices of the men hushed. Those who had their backs to me turned their heads to stare. I could have forced them to make way for me. I could have skirted the crowd but still held firm to that side of the street. Instead, I lowered my eyes and crossed to the other side.

I heard a man say something, then snicker. The others joined in. I thought of the men in my father's factory in Brazil, nodding and smiling as he passed. I'd been proud, then, that they thought so well of him, but now I wondered, as I hurried beyond the strikers' range, if those workers would have one day turned against him too.

A smell of smoke snaked after me. Someone must have put a match to the straw. I told myself I shouldn't, I wouldn't, but, still, I looked. Between the clustered bodies of the men I glimpsed flames flashing up the straw man's legs, up his arms, across his face.

And it strikes me now, a dream I've had since I was little. There's a tall building, a skyscraper only partly built, the upper storeys a skeleton of metal girders, and my father is standing near the top, framed in steel, his legs spread wide apart, his arms reaching skyward, like Charles Atlas or some evangelist. He is naked, though his intimate parts are not apparent to me. The building is in flames and he stands silhouetted against the fire, tongues of red and gold licking up his arms, flashing from his outstretched hands, his mouth open, and although I know somehow that he feels nothing, I see him scream.

I almost drop the gun. I pause on the grass to steady my hands, staring down at what I hold so that I don't have to meet the eyes of my father and his friend who have risen from their chairs. They mustn't see my tears.

—Well, it's about time, my father says.

I hand over the gun. He flips the chamber open, tips the bullets into his hand, then fits them back in place and snaps the chamber shut.

—Who first? he asks.

— Ladies first, his friend replies, bowing gallantly to me.

I don't want to shoot the gun, yet all my life I've done as I've been told. I rarely argue with what he wants. It's true, in recent months I've gone my own way, more and more, but I have not yet defied him openly.

—Come on, my father's friend teases. —If you can smuggle a gun, you should be able to shoot.

My father puts the gun into my hand, closes my fingers around the stock. He raises my arm level with my shoulder and swings it to point at the empty bottle his friend has set on the middle post of the back fence.

—Sight along the muzzle, my father says, his mouth close to my ear. His arm extends along my arm, his hand cradles mine. —Breathe in. Hold your breath. Pull the trigger. Try to hit the glass.

Out of the corner of my eye, I see my mother watching. She is standing in the kitchen doorway, holding open the screen. Her apron flutters in the breeze. If she speaks, I cannot hear her, but her phrases come to mind: If you can't say something nice, don't say anything at all. And, There but for the grace of God go thee, remember that.

I take a breath. I close my eyes.

— Go on. Shoot.

If I intend to refuse, I must speak now.

I swallow. I feel a tightness at my throat, the weight of steel against my thigh, the wrinkled skin of my father's cheek as it leans against mine.

My finger finds the trigger, pulls it slowly to.

The explosion seems to take forever, long enough to forget what it was I might have said.

NOSSA SENHORA DOS REMÉDIOS

—◆—

That I can't bear the sound of the sea comes down to this: the teacup of Miss Barbosa.

Miss Barbosa swept into my life, large and loud, not lovely but alluring with her bright-red lips and matching fingernails, red of tooth and claw like some mythical beast. I loved her swiftly and without reserve.

—To-day, she said, pronouncing each syllable separately and carefully, as if it were ripe to bursting. —To-day we will sketch the au-ber-gine.

She held the fruit aloft, her vermilion nails jewelled clasps on the dark amethyst skin, and she announced the word again, the *rrr*s trilling off her tongue, reverberating through her lips. —Au-ber-gine.

She set the eggplant on a grey velvet cloth she'd draped over a stool. Beside the eggplant, a cluster of guavas from the tree in the schoolyard and a carambola, sliced crosswise, a pear-soft yellow star.

As we pulled out our sketch pads and pencils, she glided up and down the aisles, weaving her fragrance, unimaginable blossoms tinged with Russian cigarettes, between our desks. She paused to rub her palm in the arch of a young girl's back.

— Loose! she proclaimed. — To draw, your bo-dy must be loose!

And she motioned us to our feet, set our arms swinging in great circles over our heads, then at our sides, until we were all giggling and flapping like ungainly, self-conscious butterflies.

— Close your eyes. Feel your bo-dy, feel it sway. Let your spir-it loose. You poor chil-dren, cooped up like this. Move! Dance! Pir-ou-ette!

And she twirled across the front of the grade-five class-room, her high-heeled slip-ons kicked skidding into the corner, the blue-and-gold pattern of her dress swirling wildly, lifting like waves as her arms surged back and forth above her head.

I abandoned myself to Miss Barbosa, for she was my second love. Miss Goetz was my first: a small, prim woman from a different country altogether, a woman given to narrow, belted skirts and sensible black shoes with square heels and laces that she tied in thin, perfect bows. Every morning, she would inspect our fingernails, moving along the rows of out-stretched palms, tapping my wrist approvingly as I sang with all my heart, Good morning, dear teacher, good morning to you. And every afternoon, as the big hand hit the 12 of four o'clock, she would slap her ruler on her desk and say, Class dismissed. At that very instant I'd pull open the classroom door and hold it while the other grade ones and twos filed through, the pair of us, Miss Goetz and I, in perfect unison, as if my hands were of her body, and her thoughts, inside my head.

She could have been my mother's sister, my father's second wife. I imagined Miss Goetz at our dinner table, napkin flat across her lap, her back straight the way my father liked, passing bowls of peas and diced carrots and whipped potatoes properly to the right, taking some of everything (though never more than she could finish), and cleaning every last morsel from her plate, knowing without having to be told what it meant to the starving children in Africa.

Miss Barbosa was wild and unpredictable, as different from my family and from Miss Goetz as aubergine from canned peas. Even her name, Sonia, was unlike anything I'd ever heard, the first syllable rhyming with bone, and with roan, which was precisely the colour of her long, dark hair. As much as I sometimes missed the calm order I had known in Canada with Miss Goetz, I was older now and more adventuresome, keened to the exotic. Lying in my bed at night, I would whisper their names, Lillian, Sonia, Sonia, Sonia, Lillian, and my skin would prickle with forbidden pleasure, repeating the given names of these two women, the convoluted consonants of one lending sweeter fullness to the low vowels of the other.

– Now, my dear chil-dren, are we loose? Loose in o-ur bo-dies? Yes? Then, let us draw!

Miss Barbosa passed by our desks as we drew the aubergine. Now and then, she paused to speak quietly to one student or another, urging each of us to feel the aubergine, to touch it with our eyes and hold it in our hearts, before we let it slip perfectly from our fingers to the page.

I stroked the dark skin with my gaze; I took it in, made it mine. I could do this, and more. Things I had never spoken of to anyone, things I knew Miss Barbosa would understand. How, sometimes in the night, I would leave my body on the bed and drift weightless on a silver thread, my limbs swelling until I filled the room, wall to wall. Like an angel trying out her wings, I let myself rise a little farther each time, exhilarated, engorged with spirit, my body a husk curled on the sheet below.

I did not soar according to my whim. I only flew when the cards, the first time I played them, came out right. The deck was tiny, small enough to conceal inside my closed fist. I'd made it myself from my mother's best stationery, cutting the stiff paper into fifty-two identical cards. I worked the back of each one in an elaborate interlace design, copied the fronts faithfully from the deck my parents used to play bridge. Every night I would smooth my pillow and lay down a row of seven cards, precisely spaced and squared, for a game of Solitaire. Black on red, red on black; three turns through the deck. If I won, I flew. If not, I'd play game after game until the cards of each suit were ordered on their aces, and only then would I sleep.

I moved my pencil round and round the aubergine's taut oval. Through the scrape of lead on paper, I listened to my little sister wail. She cried the whole day through. Her whimper would start as soon as she saw the high pink wall of the Escola Americana. At the gate, she would refuse to enter, and the two of us would stand like boulders in a river as the other children flowed around us, laughing and calling to one another. Day after day, I'd bribe her with promises of stories and games, explain to her that she had no choice, that she had to go to school, until finally I'd have to grab her by the arm and pull her to Miss Mary's door, to the room behind Miss Barbosa's, where her pout would shatter and the thin wail begin that would go on for hours.

— Such a small au-ber-gine! Poor thing.

Miss Barbosa stood beside me, the two of us enveloped in her scent. She tore the page from my book and let it drift to the floor.

— Please, for me, start again. With big pencil lines. Let your aubergine be large. A grand aubergine!

She sculpted the air with one hand, conjuring.

— A bold aubergine. Bigger than life!

I bent to the empty page, determined to please. She spoke more softly then, close by my cheek. — Stay after school a moment, won't you, dear?

It wasn't just me. There were four of us. Three other girls dawdled by their desks after class too. We were invited to take a trip. To the beach at Ipanema. Four days at her brother's apartment in Rio de Janeiro, where from the windows, she said, we would hear the sea.

My family lived in an apartment, on the eighth floor. The building stood on white pillars, as if on tiptoe, overlooking a

city square lined with royal palms and planted with gardens
that were traced through with narrow paths, all leading to the
white bandstand at the centre. The front of the building, and
therefore one entire wall of our apartment, floor to ceiling,
was made of glass. On windy days, the palms would brush
against the windowpanes. Sometimes, when I rose earlier
than anyone else to revel in the blue light of the *madrugada*,
that magic time before dawn, I would sit on the living-room
floor, eye to eye with the fat thrushes that rattled among
the palm leaves, whistled and preened in front of the giant
looking-glass.

During the day, the back balcony was mine. It wasn't a
balcony so much as a narrow passageway behind the kitchen
that connected a tiny bathroom with what would have been
the maid's room had my father been able to convince my
mother to hire help. Instead, it was my playroom, and for the
most part mine alone, for the back balcony was off-limits to
my little sister and scorned by the older girls, who preferred
to lie on their beds swooning to the songs of Pat Boone.

It was in the maid's room that I made my puppets, according to the directions on the Gestetnered sheet Miss Barbosa
handed out. I mixed white glue with sawdust that my father
brought me from his factory, then shaped balls of the sticky
mess around the ends of toilet-paper tubes. I pressed in eye
sockets with my thumbs, pinched ridges for noses, added
pencil-point nostrils and lips with the flat edge of a knife.
As I finished each puppet, I set it on the neck of an empty
guaraná bottle, until my whole sawdust family, mother,

father, and four children, stood in a row on glass pikes like pygmy victims of some violent coup. But the dough was too soft: the puppets' features sagged. No sooner were their expressions fixed to my satisfaction than I had to start again, moving from head to head, restoring the furrows to the father's brow, lifting the droop of the mother's eyes.

I had moved the sawdust family from the maid's room to the balcony with the hope that the sun would set their shapes, and I was fussing with them, using the knife to define one child-puppet's smile, when I glimpsed the angel flying.

She had black hair, wild about her face, as if she lay upon a pillow. Her skirt billowed green against the white-hot sky. Her arms were outstretched, as if reaching to embrace. She looked at me. Her hand, I thought, lifted slightly in a wave.

I dropped the puppet and rushed to the railing. She was nowhere in sight. I peered across the red-tile rooftops and between the jumble of tall buildings, craned my neck to look high in the sky where an angel might have soared. I hardly thought to look down, but there she was, lying on the cobblestones, her skirt still fluttering, hair streaming across her face, limbs oddly askew, one arm raised.

I stared down at the gathering crowd, men and women scurrying toward her from every which way, their thin wails like sirens rising to where I stood, my own voice in my ears, my sisters there, too, pulling at me, prying my fingers from the railing, saying, Don't look, don't look. But it was too late.

Miss Barbosa's brother lived on the fourth floor.

– High enough to muffle the noise of the traffic, Miss Barbosa said as we got into the elevator. – Low enough that we'll be able to hear waves break on the shore.

The drive to Rio de Janeiro had taken most of the day. I was not invited to sit in the front of Miss Barbosa's car, so I took the place behind the driver's seat where, if I leaned forward, I could feel her hair on my cheek and smell her skin. I kept my eyes on the mirror, in case she glanced my way. She had met us in the schoolyard just as the sky began to lighten, and by the time we skirted the curve of beach at Ipanema, it was late afternoon, the sky like pale silk smoothed above the green-glass sea.

At the door to the apartment, Miss Barbosa's brother wrapped his arms around his sister with a cry of joy and pulled her inside, kissing her loudly on her cheeks and lips.

I could not bear to look at him. He was hardly as tall as I, yet his body seemed borrowed from a much bigger man, except for the legs, which were so bony and stunted that they surely would have snapped under the weight of his torso had it not been for the metal braces strapped to them.

I had seen such a man before, in the Igreja de Nossa Senhora dos Remédios where, before I was charged with my little sister's care, I would stop on my way home from school. The heavy, carved doors of the church were always open. It was dark and quiet and cool inside. I would slip onto a bench near the back, hoping no one had noticed that I failed to trace the holy cross upon my chest. Leaning back my head, I would stare into the soaring vault painted sapphire and sprinkled with gilt like a twilit sky, and it was then that the angels spoke to me.

My mother called the church we went to every Sunday the house of God, and that was how it seemed to me, just a house. Four square walls, plain and white except for the wooden cross that hung above the choir. There, no one talked of angels. But I had read the Bible, every parchment page between its white leather covers, four a day, five on Sunday, for one whole year, and so I knew the truth: angels were everywhere. An angel guarded the Tree of Knowledge after Adam and Eve saw their nakedness. Angels warned Lot's wife and daughters not to look back or they'd turn to salt. An angel told Moses how to part the Red Sea. An angel gave Mary the news that she'd be the mother of the Son of God. And an angel, "his countenance like lightning," rolled back the stone of the sepulchre and rescued Christ from the grave.

In the Igreja Nossa Senhora dos Remédios, angels flew above the altar. They floated on the walls and dallied at the ceiling. Nossa Senhora herself stood on a cloud of angels' heads, her Virgin-blue gown brushing their brows. Some of the angels were painted gold; most were carved in wood the colour of cinnamon or in grey-green stone. Their hands were raised in greeting or folded under their chins, their gauzy robes drifting modestly about their legs, wings flaring at their backs, hair wafting in some light, celestial breeze. Although the angels in the Bible seemed always to be men, the angels in Igreja Nossa Senhora dos Remédios were clearly female though they had no breasts, which meant they were girls like me.

Often when I stopped at the church, I saw a man with shrunken legs in black braces resting against the altar rail, his head bowed in prayer. Once, he stretched forward and pressed his fingers against the Virgin's hem, and when he left, I crept to the altar rail too. What I had taken for embroidery painted on her robes was a filigree of tiny silver charms. Lips, hands, legs, even hearts. I understood, without being told, what he had done: offered a miniature likeness of his afflicted body-part in exchange for a miracle. It shamed me to think it, but I knew his prayer would not be answered. He would always have those withered legs.

To me, though, the angels whispered promises of bound-less change, flesh made spirit, spirit made flesh, again and again.

— I-pa-nema, said Miss Barbosa. — It's an old, old word, from the Indians, from before the Portuguese arrived and built the city of Rio de Janeiro. Ipanema means 'bad waters.' The waves here are very high, and the undertow is strong. You may walk on the beach and play, but you may not swim. The sea god will have no sacrifice from us today!

My heart sank. Other than my bathing suit, I had only the sundresses my mother had insisted I bring. The other girls wore halters and shorts. They played tag with the waves, teasing the retreating tide, while I stayed out of reach on the soft, dry sand.

We walked, Miss Barbosa and I, along the sweep of white beach, the sea on one side, a stockade of skyscrapers on the other, and, rising above the concrete barrier, jutting hills, which wavered darkly in the heat. We dangled our sandals from our fingers and strolled under skies blown with restless kites, past castle-builders, and lovers wrapped in each other's arms, past brawling children, *cariocas* beating samba rhythms on the hoods of cars, and vendors selling *guaraná*, spun sugar, pineapples sliced open with machetes, and rows of *figas,* the Brazilian good-luck charm, tiny fists carved from coloured quartz, black against evil spirits, green for hope.

Miss Barbosa paused and faced the waves. She seemed to be listening for something above the tumult of the beach, then she turned to me.

–Do you know, my dear, why it is the sea moans?

I shook my head.

– It is an old Brazilian tale. It involves a princess, of course. A young girl, much like you. This princess, she loved to sit in her garden and watch the changing beauty of the sea. She was always alone, and although the sea was very beautiful, she longed for some living company. 'I am so very lonely,' she sighed aloud one day, and suddenly out of the sea arose a beautiful serpent, not frightening at all, but lovely, and kind. 'I am La-bis-mena and I have come to play,' the serpent said. And every day thereafter the princess and Labismena played, although the serpent disappeared the moment anyone else came near.

Miss Barbosa looked again toward the sea and I followed her gaze. The waves slid like quicksilver, chasing their shadows to the shore. We waited, as if Labismena herself might raise her lovely head.

– The years passed happily until, one day, the serpent looked at the princess with sorrow in her eyes and said, 'Dear princess, you are growing older. We cannot play together any more. But, remember, I will always be your friend. If ever you are in trouble, come to the sea and call my name.'

– The princess, by this time, was old enough to marry. Her father was a practical man, and soon he arranged for his daughter to become the wife of a king who lived nearby. He was very rich, but this king was also very old. The princess wept bitterly. She thought her heart would break, for she had imagined another sort of life for herself. Then she remembered her friend and she rushed to the sea, calling, 'Labismena, Labismena.'

Miss Barbosa cupped her hands around her lips and rolled the syllables toward the waves. – La-bis-mena. La-bis-mena.

No one on the beach seemed to take notice but me.

– The serpent heard the princess call and immediately she appeared, just as she had said she would. She knew why the princess had summoned her, and already she had a plan, one that would save the princess from the ancient king and unite her with a prince who would be her one true love. 'In return, dear friend, please do one thing for me,' begged the serpent. 'At the moment of your greatest happiness, on the day that you are wed, call out my name three times, for that will break my enchantment and I will become the princess I once was.'

– The princess promised, with all her heart. The serpent kept her word, and so the princess escaped the fate her father had devised for her. Soon she met a handsome prince who asked her to be his bride, but on the day that they were married, when she was as happy as she would ever be, the princess forgot her promise to the serpent. She did not call Labismena's name.

– And so Labismena lost her chance to be transformed. She remained forever a serpent trapped in the sea, where she lives to this day, and with every wave that breaks upon the shore, you can hear her sad yearning, her *saudade*, in the moaning of the sea.

The selfishness of the princess stung my heart. That evening, I did everything I could think of to prove that I would never be such a thoughtless friend. I offered to help make dinner. I set the table for us all. I repacked my suitcase, stowing my things neatly away. While we waited to eat, I suggested games that we might play, but the other girls preferred to chatter together on the beds, eating the Hershey bars they'd brought, so I went into the living room, where I sat quietly, not too far from Miss Barbosa and her brother, who leaned together on the railing of the balcony to catch the evening's ocean breeze. I wanted to tell them that they might see angels, that I had once seen an angel fly, but they talked to each other in low voices of things I couldn't understand.

When the maid announced dinner, the girls came into the room, one of them carrying a cake wrapped in foil that she handed to Miss Barbosa.

—How thoughtful! Miss Barbosa exclaimed, drawing the girl to her in a hug. —We'll have it after dinner, with our tea.

The girl who'd brought the banana loaf sat in the place of honour at Miss Barbosa's right-hand side. I was shown to the other end of the table, to a chair beside her brother where I had to concentrate to keep my foot from accidentally touching his leg.

It was when the maid brought the teapot to the table that I saw my chance.

—I'll pour! I said, leaping up.

Miss Barbosa did not say no. She looked at me with the smallest of smiles and nodded to the maid, who set the pot in front of me. I remembered what my mother had taught me: the eldest and most honoured woman first. I picked up the teapot with one hand, supported the spout with the other, and walked carefully around the table to where Miss Barbosa sat. The teapot was large and very heavy, but I could manage, I was certain. I had skills that no one knew about. I could do nine things at once: tap one foot, hold the other up off the floor, snap the fingers of one hand while slapping my thigh with that wrist and tapping my cheek with the other hand, wag my head side to side, blinking, humming, and flaring my nostrils, all at the same time.

The tea was pouring smoothly, flowing into Miss Barbosa's cup. The china was a lovely colour of blue. It had a rim of gold, and when I bent forward I could see in the bottom of the cup a tiny painted angel, flying. I looked up at Miss Barbosa then, and saw how her dark hair streamed across her face as she looked down at me. Dark, dark hair, wild about her face, like the angel I'd seen flying, the one that lay spread against the cobblestones, one arm raised.

The room shifted at just that moment and the tea was on my hand, the cup on the floor, hot tea splashing everywhere, on the table, down my dress, on the shards of blue china, the broken angel on the floor.

Miss Barbosa should have come to me. She should have wrapped me in her arms, pressed her lips against the scalded skin of my palm.

But she just sat there, glaring, at me, at the broken cup. My mother's cup, my mother's best cup, was all she could say, and in her eyes I saw Miss Goetz, her thin arms folded against her chest as she stared down at the girl who wiped at the vomit she'd spewed on the classroom floor.

It was Miss Barbosa's brother who smoothed butter on my hand. He wrapped it in gauze, murmuring all the while, —Never mind, dear. Never mind. Such things happen.

We were all sent to bed then, but I could not sleep. The skin of my hand, under its bandage, throbbed with every breath. I closed my eyes and tried to free myself from the body that lay on the bed, tried to find the silver thread that let me fly, prayed to the angels to help me leave this place.

But no angels whispered back to me. All I heard were the waves that broke against the sand, and in that sad, relentless rhythm, Labismena's *saudade,* her yearning for her friend.

—⁓—

All of this comes back to me in a basement four thousand miles away, in the centre of this northern country, as distant from any sea as I can be. Perhaps it is the smell of damp that reminds me, or the woman I saw fall today from the top of another building, her body exploding on the sidewalk like a too-ripe fruit. Later, when I passed the place again, a man in uniform was hosing the asphalt, flushing small red bits of flesh into the gutter.

I stand here all but naked. My breasts are exposed. I wear only a long cotton skirt that catches on my hips, made wide by the passage of two sons. The flimsy fabric reveals the shape of my thighs, my pubic mound. One foot is placed in front of the other so that I seem to step forward. My arms are not stretched back like wings (I might like such a pose), they are raised and crossed above my head, caught inside my top as if I were just taking off my clothes.

—Lean into it more, my husband says.

And I do, for still I strive to please.

—No, he says, irritably. —Not like that. Not your whole body. Just your face, so I can see its contours through the cloth.

I press my forehead, my nose, and my lips into the fabric, breathing in my own scent and the smell of the cotton, its fibres, its dyes, its many washings. I will stand like this for hours as my husband, the artist, massages the clay with his hands, searching for a likeness of me.

Inside the cloth, my breath washes over me like a tide, and I think of the angels, of Miss Barbosa, of Labismena and Nossa

Senhora dos Remédios. Of how these women, disembodied, drift with me. I stop myself from thinking of silver threads in lonely bedrooms, of balconies and broken cups, bits of flesh in a gutter or limbs oddly askew; of my body exposed and my face smothered, my breath like the sea, a sad lament.

THE BLUE OF THE *MADRUGADA*

—◠—

The train can't move fast enough. I scoop it up, fling it over my shoulder like a feather boa, and take off down the track, bending my head into the west wind, spine flattened by the strength of my stride, like a speed skater or a quarterback. I pummel the rails, growing bigger with every step, the forest a puddle-splashed carpet tickling my toes as I pass, leaping across the prairie to slouch against the first mountain slope, sliding the train back to its track, drawing my hand alongside the cars, aligning them on the rails, hardly out of breath at all.

I open my eyes.

In the half-light of the railway car, the window reflects me back to myself, a round-faced girl with hair cropped short to contain the frizz, with big eyes and full lips that don't quite close over that protruding front tooth. As often as I look in the mirror (too often, my mother says: Pride goeth before a fall), what I see still confounds me. Where is that brawny Amazon, that brilliant Ayn Rand acolyte who lives and breathes inside my head?

I press against the faulty reflection to see beyond the glass. Since the train turned north from Union Station, there have been trees and more trees, interrupted only rarely by a lake or an outcropping of rock. At first, the landscape bolstered my mood. This was where my family spent two weeks every summer in a rented cottage. When the maples gave way at last to pine and fir, my parents would look at each other and smile, the air inside the car softening so suddenly that in the back seat my sisters and I would stop bickering and break into our ritual song, "Off to the beach, oh what fun! School days are over and holidays begun. . . ."

The tune irks me now. So does this family snapshot. I'm not part of that any more.

I grow impatient with the reel of conifers. I want grass-land. I want mountains, storm-chiselled rock faces, and gullies that finger dead riverbeds. I want sloughs and buttes. Impenetrable chasms. Shrouded heaths and braes and bogs that cradle corpses for centuries. Monsoon-raked atolls, churning fjords, reefs, and archipelagos. Paths of my own making underfoot. The mistral, the sirocco, the tramontane in my hair. I want what I've never known, and more: what I can't imagine yet.

Relax. You only left Toronto a few hours ago. It's still two days to Calgary.

I say this out loud. Talking to myself is proof that I am alone. It also runs in the family. In the train's insistent rhythm

I hear my father mumbling as he putters in the basement with his electric train, the locomotive thrumming past tiny perfect bungalows, past woodlots of identical trees, his words circling up through the heating ducts to my room, unintended messages, unwanted, indecipherable.

I hoist myself a little to look around, caring after all whether the other passengers have heard me. The train isn't even half full. The family across the way is dozing. I hear snores from the man in the seat in front of me. The aisles are deserted as far as I can see.

It is almost midnight. I dig into the travelling bag wedged between my legs and the window, feeling for crackers and cheese. Each day's food is wrapped separately, a trick to maintain discipline. I'm not just being frugal: I'm counting on this journey to pare some flesh from my hips. I'll never again have to walk the gauntlet of the school bus, past the boys who call me Lard-Ass, but I don't want that hateful nickname to spring to anyone else's lips.

I hesitate a moment, then open the packet for day two.

Cheddar cheese, Stoned Wheat crackers, McIntosh apples: the three basic food groups. For vegetables, I buy V8 juice from the porter, a handsome black music student who is working on the trains for the summer. I've never talked to a black person before. I think he likes me; he finds reasons to stop and lean against my seat. I like him too. Now, at the sound of his eager step in the aisle, I lick my lips to make them glisten, run a surreptitious finger along my eyebrows, smoothing wayward hairs. Something in the gesture recalls my mother, whisking off her apron at the sound of my father's car pulling into the garage. But, I reassure myself, this is not the same at all.

– How about a good-night kiss? the porter says with a wink as he dims the lights.

I laugh and blow an exaggerated pucker his way. He pretends to catch it and blows one back to me as he leaves the railway car.

I suck on a crumb of cheese and let my mind slide to kisses, soft kisses on my lips, kisses dabbling my ear, my neck, my breast. My nipples tingle with the memory of those wet, licking kisses, a resonance between my legs, too, as I remember the day before I left, that pearly glistening on the dark weave of my pubic hair. I had let my boyfriend go that far.

We decided he wouldn't come to the station to see me off. It would break our hearts, we said, although the truth is I was afraid my mother would see on our faces what we'd been up to on the basement couch. This trip to Alberta to visit my sister is a graduation gift from my parents, but I see it as a clean break between my past and my future, which will begin in September when I enrol at the University of Western Ontario. I think of my father, my mother, and my little sister on the station platform in Toronto and, in my memory, I place my boyfriend there too, all of them waving, becoming smaller as the distance between us widens. I watch them diminish, first dwarfs, then dolls, then miniature figurines. I think, There is no limit to how small, how insignificant people can become.

I unfold the train blanket and curl up under the coarse, grey cloth, pulling it to my chin. My hands, tucked between

my legs, cup my pubic mound, then slip inside my slacks: a
tiny, tender touch, hardly a movement at all, the blanket at
my mouth now, to muffle my ragged breaths, one finger on
that warm slick swelling, rubbing, circling, stroking until the
ripe bud bursts, pulsing such sweetness through my belly, my
breasts, my thighs, each surge from that flexing centre steady-
ing my heart, soothing me, as always, at last, to sleep.

–You sleep with your mouth hanging open.

The porter is staring down at me as I wake on the last
morning. The kindness that gentled his gaze during the past
two days is gone. His voice has a cruel edge to it, and I sit up
suddenly, remembering the night before when he forced
open the bathroom door as I tried to slide it closed, squeezed
into the narrow space with me, the sink a sharp line against
my spine as he kissed me hard on the mouth, groped in the
folds of my sweater, twisted and kneaded the breast he found,
pried apart my teeth with his tongue. –Come on, you know
you want to, it's our last chance, he hissed, sucking at my
neck, both hands now on my breasts. – No I don't, I said,
holding in tears. – Please stop! Back in my seat, huddled
under double blankets, I braced my feet against the seat in
front of me, tensed my body for his step in the aisle. I had led
him on. I hadn't meant to. Still, there was no harm done, he
had let me go.

I shake off the memory and push past the porter, ignoring him as I hurry to gather my things. The train is slowing
to a crawl; we are entering Calgary station. As I step down to

the platform, to my oldest sister's waiting arms, it is not the incident itself but the porter's words as I awakened that I carry with me. The uninvited intimacy of being watched while I slept is hard enough to bear, but he could have done anything to me then, slowly pulled aside the blanket, touched his finger to my bare skin. The moment belongs to him, that's what I can't abide.

As we drive from the train station through downtown Calgary, I see the city's past strewn in heaps on street corners. Cranes poke at the sky, raising girders half-clad in shiny, coloured glass. The city appeals to me immediately, not the promise of what's to come but the boom and clutter of construction, the restless dust. At last, I think, I've arrived at a place where things are happening.

My sister lives with her husband and new baby in an apartment complex in the suburbs. When my mother arranged for me to stay with her, it didn't occur to me to ask where I would sleep. It is apparent as soon as we enter. A double bed and a bassinet fill the only bedroom. I take one look at the pull-out couch in the living room and decide that as soon as I find a job I'll get a place of my own.

Over the next few days, I establish my routine. My sister is busy with the baby; her husband, a parole officer, is mostly at work. I spend the mornings with the telephone book, working through the listings of newspapers, libraries, and bookstores. Everywhere the answer is the same: No summer help needed, thanks.

In the afternoons, while the baby sleeps and my sister cleans and bakes, I sunbathe on the square of lawn between the apartment buildings. It is only the end of May, but the concrete has concentrated the sun's heat in the little grassy common, making it deliciously hot. My bathing suit is bright yellow splashed with big black daisies, a two-piece that caused my mother to suck in her breath when I emerged from the change room. I was appalled, too, but for a different reason. Seen in the shop mirror, under the scrutiny of the salesgirl, my thighs seemed to bulge from the leg openings like dimpled white sausages.

– Do you see how men look at you? my mother said as we left the store. I turned to her sharply, my defences ready. But she was smiling. – You're very pretty, you know.

One afternoon, as I arrange my transistor radio, my book, and a bottle of Fanta orange on the grass, I notice that scaffolding has been erected on one of the buildings. I ease myself, belly-down, on my towel, reaching back to unhook my top and slide the straps off my shoulders, taking extra care to tuck my breasts under me, securely out of sight. I read for a while then doze, dreaming through half-closed eyes that the walls around me are an Andean village and the workers who are whitewashing on the scaffolding, a band of guerillas, Che's men, waiting to strike a blow for justice and freedom.

One of the workers walks toward me. I watch his shoes approach. They are white. His socks are white too. And his pants. I think of hospitals, Ontario Hospitals, asylums for the insane.

– Hi. My name's John.

I'm trapped. I can't get up without letting go of the strip of cloth I clutch to my breasts.

—This is going to sound strange, he begins, pausing for so long that I have time to imagine everything except what comes next. —The thing is, I'm a painter. I'm just doing these buildings to earn some money, but really I paint on canvas, with acrylics and oils. I saw you lying here and, well, I just wanted to ask if you'd model for me.

He stops politely, to allow me a response, but I can't think of a thing to say.

—Look, he continues at last. —You don't have to worry. I have a wife, and a little boy. My wife usually models for me but she's pregnant again, and I want a different body. To paint, I mean. You're just right for what I have in mind. A girl who's almost a woman. You are a woman already, of course, I didn't mean you're a little girl or anything like that, but . . . well, I just think you'd be perfect.

—I don't know, I say slowly, hedging for time.

—You don't have to make up your mind right now. Think about it. I'll give you my phone number, he says, digging a piece of paper and a pencil out of his pocket.

As he writes, I fold my arms closer over my cleavage. The way he looks at me, not like the boys I've known, but with appreciation and genuine interest, excites me more than if he'd propositioned me. I've let boys touch me and kiss me, baring one part of me at a time, but no one has seen me entirely without clothes, not since I've developed this new body with its swellings, its hidden folds and grooves, that dark, furred shield. I am secretly proud of the generous curves of my figure. They seem acceptable, even attractive to me, glimpsed in private in the bathroom mirror, freed from the constriction of girdle and brassiere. To stand utterly naked, to be stared at for hours, chastely, without touching: the thought dazzles me.

Nothing, none of my mother's lectures, not my sisters' smug reports on the ways of boys, not even the scrawled intelligences I struggle to decipher in public washrooms, has prepared me for this.

He lays the scrap of paper on the grass by my book.

– Here's my number. Call and talk to my wife. She'll tell you I'm serious. I'm not coming on to you or anything. I can't pay you, but I could give you one of the rough sketches.

I have to say something. I don't want him to think I'm a prude.

– I'll let you know, I manage finally, cringing at the little girl's voice that leaks out.

– I'll be waiting, he says.

I smile goodbye and he strolls back to his scaffolding as though what's just happened is the most ordinary thing in the world, as though we've been passing the time of day, discussing something perfectly commonplace, like babysitting for his son, not me taking off my clothes, baring my breasts and my pale curving bum to a married man I've never in my life laid eyes on before.

I turned down the painter: my sister wouldn't hear of it. If I knew her better, I might have been able to figure out how to talk her into it, or at least how to sneak behind her back. But she left for boarding school when I was only ten. We hardly know each other at all.

She takes a closer interest in me now. When I hang up the telephone, she insists on a report of the jobs I've called about and, when I go out to apply at a convenience store or a fast-food restaurant, she quizzes me on the details of how it went.

I don't know what she is worried about. It's not as if I absolutely have to have a job. I already have a scholarship for university, given to me by a private benefactor. I call him my "sugar daddy." I don't mean any disrespect, really. This is how I speak of him to my friends, the insinuation dulling, I hope, the gloss of my good fortune. Achievement, I've learned, is suspect; shared hardship makes a better footing for friendship.

My sugar daddy once owned the factory where my father is a manager. When he sold it, he set up a scholarship for employees' sons to study engineering at a nearby university. In the spring, I'd written to him:

> *I am a daughter who wants to study English.*
> *I want, one day, to write. I'm an A student, and*
> *no boys from the village are graduating this year.*
> *Won't you give me the scholarship instead?*

He replied by inviting me to his house for an interview. Lawns surrounded his stone mansion like a park. A house-keeper showed me to a room so thick with books that I peered around for several minutes before I saw him, a thin little man, impossibly old, sitting in an armchair, awash in newsprint. He motioned me to the leather chair beside him, and almost immediately began his interrogation, asking what I'd read, what I was reading, what I intended to read; the kind of writing I liked and the kind I hoped to do. I thought it was a test. I tried to shape my answers, naming Thomas Hardy, George Eliot, Margaret Laurence, not admitting my obsession with Thomas B. Costain and, uncertain of my ground, keeping Ayn Rand and Sylvia Plath to myself.

We spent the afternoon in his library. He said little, but listened to me intently. Now and then, he pulled a book from the shelves that lined every wall, floor to ceiling. My family's books would hardly fill one corner: the Bible, *Pears Cyclopaedia*, my mother's old nursing texts, several hymnals, a biography of Norman Bethune, picture books of Muskoka and old Toronto. What we read came from the public library or from friends, I suppose. (Where else would my mother have got the bent and curling copy of *Fanny Hill* I found during one of my forays into her bedside table?)

I hadn't known that one person could own so many books. It seemed faintly sinful, hoarding all these stories, these times and places, having so much understanding and inspiration at one's own beck and call. It seemed especially odd for a man. In my family, and in the library where I spent my Saturday afternoons, it was mostly women who read books, and it was men (my father, uncles, visitors) who said to me, their disapproval tinged with disgust: You've always got your nose in a book!

I coveted this man's library, all these books. I wanted to get up and touch each one, let my fingers drift along their spines, breathe deeply of all that ink and paper and leather binding. I contented myself with what he handed down to me: Boswell, Milton, Herodotus, Cicero, Defoe. Some names I recognized, most I didn't, though I pretended to as I struggled to make a mental list. I'd almost forgotten why I'd been invited there, when he said, –Yes, I'll give you the scholarship.

I was to work in the summers and save what I could; he would pay the rest, for as long as I wanted to stay in school. This was more than I had bargained for. I hadn't really thought beyond first year. My future I defined only in negatives: not a teacher, not a nurse, not a wife. In my heart of hearts, yes, a writer, although when he asked, I'd been at a loss to say what exactly I meant by that or how I thought I might go about it.

–One more thing, he said. –It is my view that a person is not ready to join his life with another's until the age of thirty, at least. If you marry while you are still in school, my support will end.

When I told him I was spending the summer in Calgary, he gave me a letter of introduction to one of his business associates in the city. I had no intention of using it. But after three weeks, when I still don't have a job and I'm going crazy in the apartment with only my sister for company, I call up my sugar daddy's friend, and he helps me get a position in the coffee shop of his club. I learn how to make real western sandwiches, how to clean the soft-ice-cream machine, and how to balance the cash.

I work the late shift. After I close up, I sit alone in the deserted room, on the customer's side of the counter, sipping coffee and pretending I'm a member of the club too, the daughter of a wealthy oilman, perhaps. I practise the languid movements I've watched throughout the evening, the casual way the girls sit, their legs crossed high at the thigh, not modestly at the ankle as I've been taught to do. They look so at ease in their slim, tanned bodies, so certain that things will always go their way. Rich enough to make mistakes. Rich enough not to care.

And so, late one night when my boyfriend calls the club, I am absorbed in my charade, literally not quite myself. I haven't heard from him since I left home almost a month ago, yet I am disappointed at the sound of his voice, annoyed, in fact, as though confronted with something I thought I'd left behind.

But none of this explains the outrageous lie I hear myself tell.

My period is late, I say to him, and I listen to his panic, knowing, sort of, that what we did in the basement could not possibly have made me pregnant, but not being absolutely certain, just the same. Years ago, in Brazil, when my mother told me the facts of life, she drew precise anatomical diagrams: an egg slipping down the Fallopian tube to the womb, a sperm travelling up the vagina through the cervix to join the ovum in the uterus. In each ejaculation, five hundred million sperm, hundreds of thousands in every drop of semen, she said, and it only takes one.

The clinical facts, I knew, but if fate would have it, who's to say a single-minded spermatozoon couldn't squiggle its way from a finger, a groin, or even a towel, to my ripe and waiting egg? I, for one, believed the newspaper story about the girl who gave birth in the back seat of her parents' car in the parking lot of a mall, swearing she had no reason to think she was pregnant because she'd never had sex. And then there's the Virgin Mary, but even I am not presumptuous enough to press that point.

– My god, he says. – When will you know for sure? Should I come out there? We'll get married. Don't worry.

I thought he'd laugh and set me straight. Or maybe in the back of my mind was my mother's warning that at the first hint of pregnancy, a man will run for the hills. Either way, what I've done is inexcusable. I confess my lie.

–I never want to see you again, he says, the words coming faster to him than to me.

He slams down the phone. I should feel relieved. This is what I want.

– I broke up with my boyfriend, I tell my sister the next morning.

Since I started work, she has eased up on me, and I've become used to sleeping on the couch. We aren't friends exactly, but we've found a plateau I think I can tolerate for the six weeks still left of summer.

I sit on a stool in the narrow kitchen, sipping grapefruit juice and watching her knead bread. She slaps the dough on the counter, bears down on it with both fists, folds it over, shifts it a quarter-turn, and bears down again, no pause in her rhythm. She is the oldest of the four sisters, five years older than myself, and I view her with a mixture of awe and dismay. Awe that she left home so young, that she put herself through physiotherapy school, that she has those fine, strong hands trained to know why a body hurts and how to make it well again. Dismay that she's using her healing hands to wash dishes and knead bread.

– Have you met someone else? she asks.

I tell her about the boys at the club, rich boys who drive red Camaros and black Triumphs, sons of lawyers and doctors and accountants, the sort my mother means when she says it's as easy to marry a rich man as a poor one. And I tell her about the sports pros, men who teach badminton and tennis to the boys' mothers, old women with yellow hair and skin as brown and tough as hide. The pros flirt with me as they eat the supper I make for them, teasing each other to ask me out until finally one does, inviting me to the Red Fox for a drink.

– He obviously didn't realize I'm three years underage, I say with a laugh, neglecting to add that I did go to the bar with this man even though I suspect he's close to thirty, and married.

It is dangerous, I know, to tell half-truths. The whole truth can so easily slip out. But I have to talk to someone. Sharing little confidences with my sister lessens the pressure of holding so much in and, at the same time, creates an impression of openness, I hope. If I told her nothing at all, she'd become watchful again and, more than anything, I want my life to be my own.

So I don't tell her about my boss, who trapped me in the elevator and ran his hands up and down my body, muttering that this was part of the job. Or about the strangers who give me rides when I work late, men I thank with quick kisses. And I don't tell her that what I talk about with these men is sex, not the doing of it, of course, but at what age a girl should give up her virginity, to whom, and under what circumstances. Waiting until I am married is old-fashioned, I know, but my first time, I tell each one of them, will be with a man I truly love.

– Be careful, my sister warns, as if she's overheard my thoughts. – Men are only out for one thing.

– Not with me they're not.

I know I should just agree with her and stop this conversation, but I want to convince her that she's wrong, that I am different from her, that although we are sisters, a vast landscape stretches between us.

– We just talk. I think it's fascinating, how they see life. And even if they do have sex on the brain, it doesn't mean I do.

– Not much you don't! she says. She stops her kneading, looks steadily at me and sighs. – God, you're so naive.

– Well, I'd rather be naive than cynical.

I've gone too far. She hardens her eyes and slaps the dough back on the counter.

– I may be cynical, but from now on you'll introduce me to the men you go out with, understand?

– You're not my mother. I don't have to do what you say. If I make a mistake, I'll take the consequences. And I sure as hell won't end up like you!

The ringing of the telephone saves me.

I haven't heard this voice for three years, but I know it immediately, the slightly formal, Hello there, the soft German accent that transforms, delightfully, the most familiar words.

My friend. My pen pal. My confidant.

–Yes, I'm back in Canada. In fact, I'm in Calgary, on my way to Banff to fight forest fires. Your mother told me you were here.

I try to imagine his straight blond hair streaked with ashes, his stocky body dressed in fireman's gear. The last time I saw him was at a grade-ten dance; he was wearing blue jeans he'd made into bell-bottoms by sewing paisley fabric into the seams. We've written to each other often since he moved with his family back to Europe. Mostly he sends me postcards from places I've only read about in books: the Black Forest, the blue Danube, the house where Anne Frank hid. He crams the backs with tiny script, illuminating the margins with drawings. Instead of his name, he signs a pseudonym, ÀMA, which he uses just with me, he says. It means *à mon amie*, which I find touching, though the ambiguity of *amie*, friend or girlfriend, intrigues and puzzles me.

I quickly change into a miniskirt and wait for him on the front steps of the apartment building. When he arrives, at last, we go upstairs, I introduce him quickly to my sister, then we escape, running across the grass behind the apartments to a path that leads down the hillside toward the river. I take him to a fallen log veiled by a tangle of wild roses, a place I sometimes go to be alone. We only have a few hours before he has to leave for the mountains, yet we sit in easy silence, fingers interlocked, his thumb playing on my palm.

I have the urge to say, I love you. I have said these words before, to the boy who kissed me on the basement couch, but that boy had said them first. I had meant it then, in a way. How could I have let him do the things he did to me if we weren't in love?

But it isn't the meaning of the words so much as the way they charge the air that makes me eager to hear them again.

—Do you love me? I say.

—◊—

All the pews in the darkened church are empty. Beside me at the altar is the sweet blond boy who held my hand on that Calgary hillside almost two years ago. Behind us stand our best friends and, in front of us, the minister, a stooped man with liver-spotted fingers and high, knobby cheeks rouged with broken blood vessels. He mumbles so softly that we have to lean close to hear, holding our breath against the odour of age that rises from his clothes. He is the only clergyman we could find in four hours of walking from church to church who would agree to marry us today. We would have preferred a city official, a government employee rather than a man of the cloth, but City Hall is booked for weddings months in advance. As it is, the law has forced us to wait three days.

—They don't make it easy to be spontaneous, I muttered to the woman filling out the marriage licence forms.

—No, dear, she replied kindly. —But it gives you a chance to change your mind.

I've already had my moment's doubt, it won't happen again.

For a year after we professed our love in Calgary, we wrote to each other every day from our separate universities, both in Ontario but hundreds of miles apart. His letters were mazes I never tired of exploring: fragments of poems, exotic turns of phrase, obscure expressions bound together with delicately rendered male and female bodies, sinuously entwined. I felt moved to construct wordless labyrinths of my own, collages of picture postcards, paintings cut from books, mementoes from Brazil, which I glued together in the strange solitude of my room in the women's residence.

Sometimes, it's true, I felt the want of frank expression between us. What did it mean, really:

My little one, I love you so,
so I love you, little one, little love,
I love you just a little.

Did he love me? Was this a tender riddle? Or was it just some convoluted wordplay that I was reading too much into?

For the truth was, I was beginning to lose my faith in words. Not in their power over me: a well-wrought phrase could still thrill me or throw me into despair. No, it was my capacity for discerning meaning in words that I had begun to doubt and, more than that, my ability to shape them to my purpose. My university professors demanded a language foreign to me, a vocabulary of analysis for which, they made it clear, I showed little talent. Even in the privacy of our love letters, words sometimes made me apprehensive, left me confused, as though I had forgotten how to arrange them properly, as though I had misplaced the key to deciphering the code in what he wrote.

> If I gave you raindrops, would you hang them from your ears?

So much of his expression was like that, elegant and oblique. But then he'd write to me about his worries and his hopes in sentences so straightforward that my confidence would be restored. If, at times, I didn't understand him, I decided it must have been because he was profound.

I was, he said, his inspiration. With me, he could make great art. And so I put on the robes of the Muse, overjoyed to find this destiny, grateful to set aside my own vague ambitions, to separate myself, at last, from the beautiful young women and the brilliant young men who seemed so at home in that old Ontario university where I had not yet been able to find a place.

Do you hear what I hear? he wrote. You can stop listening now.

On the first anniversary of our Calgary rendezvous, I invited him to visit me. I had taken a summer job at a newspaper in a town less than a hundred miles from where he lived. He said he would arrive on the first bus, but all morning I waited in my apartment, the pages of Janson's *History of Art* wilting on my lap, my hair frizzing with the humidity that thickened as the hours passed. I turned the clock to the wall, tired of marking the progress of the second hand. He was late by one hour, then two. We had planned other assignations during the year, all of which had fallen through because of lack of funds or conflicting schedules or for reasons that were never explained. He'd simply failed to appear. I thought that, this time, in honour of the occasion, he would come for sure.

It was mid-afternoon when I tacked a note to my door:

> I told you the last time this happened that
> I wouldn't take it again. I've left for the day.
> You blew it, sir!

But I didn't leave. I stayed inside, heard him climbing the stairs when it was almost suppertime, knocking at the door, hopeful at first, a soft little tapping, then more insistent, and finally loudly, staccato. I sat rigid, holding my breath for fear I'd call out, listening as the footsteps receded, gripping my chair to stop myself from running after him, my heart lifting as the footsteps returned, though this time there was no knock, and by the time I understood what he was doing, he'd left for good.

Underneath my big block printing, his tiny script:

> *Eine Schwalbe macht keinen Sommer.*
> *Auch wenn ich dich liebe.*

For a long time I thought "One swallow doesn't make a summer" meant there were others he could love. It wasn't until the summer was over and I'd moved back to university that I was able to translate the second line properly: "And the same is true of my love." The words shamed me in my pettiness and absolved his breach of promise. His love was constant as the seasons; his love would endure.

My girlfriend is beautiful: thin and blonde, with spectacular legs. When she hands me the ring, our fingers bump and we smile. We've only known each other a few months, but already we've shared a lifetime of pleasure and suffering, it seems.

I've never developed a talent for friendship. I am too much with my own thoughts, which frequently baffle me. And I am too much a companion of books, where so often loose ends are neatly tied, where justice and mercy can almost always be found, and where even darkness, when it prevails, has a faintly noble sheen. I haven't quite mastered the tricky allegiances of the women's residence, the patterns of camaraderie that shift like a kaleidoscope, breaking apart at the slightest provocation, then settling again into some new configuration which, from the outside at least, seems almost the same.

With boys, too, I am wary, suspicious of their friendship, uncertain of my own desires. The misunderstanding of the past summer has made me distrust myself even more. My German sweetheart did not call after he left the note on my apartment door, and I was too hurt, too angry, then too ashamed to contact him, though I missed what we'd shared more than I would admit.

And so I was by myself, as usual, when at the beginning of second year, one of the new girls stopped me in the corridor of the residence.

–I know someone who's in love with you, she said.

She was the instrument of the fates that conspired to reunite me with my sweetheart: he had been her boyfriend's best friend for years. On the first weekend that her boyfriend drove down to visit, he brought my love to me too, and we held each other, weeping, admitting how wrong we'd been. After that, every Friday night, the boys would make the two-hour drive from their university to ours, wearing a groove in the highway, they said, straight to their girls.

She was lovely and I was bookish: we became best friends too. We sneaked cigarettes and drank bottles of wine that her older sister bought for us. We hung our bras out the window and set fire to them with our lighters, choking on the smoke and the smell of sour armpits the synthetic fibre gave off as it burned. And every weekend we sat in the window of her room and watched for her boyfriend's green Morris Minor. All four of us would squeeze into the tiny foreign car to find a cheap hotel where no one would notice that our signet rings turned band-side-out weren't really wedding rings at all. Her boyfriend, who wanted to be a singer, would bring his guitar, and we'd sit cross-legged on the sagging, iron bed, ignoring the stains on the walls and the drunken shouts from the rooms on either side, singing to each other, –'What a day for a daydream, Custom-made for a daydreamin' boy. . . .'

The boys brought beer and a little grass, which I refused to share for I hated the taste of one and the other frightened me. My state of mind was already fragile, so much so that I'd had to stop reading the bleak poets I loved, like Sylvia Plath.

I'd always been given to occasional dark thoughts, but lately I'd been hearing voices. When I showered I'd have to turn off the water every few minutes, convinced someone was whispering to me. Sometimes I could even make out the words: taunts about my body, my solitary nature, my failing marks. Then murmurs and hisses that pushed further, you're not worth anything, life's not worth anything, until, inevitably, the unthinkable: Why not just end it all.

I couldn't seem to let go of that. I thought about it all the time, exactly how it might be done. A hair dryer yanked into the bath (though I wouldn't want to be found naked and it would look odd if I wore clothes, even underwear). Pills swallowed quickly, time enough to hide the bottle and simulate a heart attack (though what kind of pills, exactly, and how many, and would there be pain?). Knives and guns were out of the question, of course, but I scanned the tallest buildings as I walked from class to class, looking for one with easy access to the roof and an asphalt surface below, insurance against survival.

The voices stopped as suddenly as they had started, on the day I decided to quit school. My girlfriend and I would finish out the year, then we'd take off for Europe, travel to our hearts' content, give my artist and her singer time to become famous on their own. The day the letter came confirming our jobs in a Middlesex hotel, we sang at the top of our lungs, dancing around my small room.

– And what sex would that be? we asked each other in mock British accents, giddy with what we dared.

We celebrated again the day our passports came, but later, alone in my bed, my face to the wall, I saw another future in my dreams. Night after night, always the same: I am a ball of clay rolling down a long, dark tunnel that at first seems smooth, then twists and turns sharply, its walls bristling with projections, knobs, and blades that cut into me. I can feel them as I roll along, unable to control the speed or direction of my progress, the knives cutting deeper, gouging flesh, carving great parts of me away, until I waken terrified that soon there will be nothing left of me.

And then, a variation: instead of clay, my body, and instead of knives, the hands and lips of men, but still the dark, silent tunnel to travel through, the prodding and gouging to endure and, always, the terror that this journey will be the end of me.

The church is so dark. Our friends carry candles in wrought-iron holders, candles of a particular, intense blue, the colour of the *madrugada*, that moment before dawn when the day still holds all its promise, a time I have loved since I was a child. I wish we could light the candles now, not just to relieve the gloom, but for the virtue of the flame.

For years I'd kept an unlit candle of this particular blue close to me, as a talisman. I have never touched a flame to it, thinking that would be like squandering the light. Never, that is, until the night my girlfriend and I waited and the boys did not arrive.

It was a Friday. We had whiled away the evening in her room drinking the wine we'd smuggled in for the weekend, our disappointment swelling to annoyance, then outrage when they failed to show up. Hours later, we crawled out the basement window to be sick on the lawn, vowing in slurred, strident voices never to see those boys again. No matter how much they begged us, we'd never take them back. Then, finally, her boyfriend called.

—There was an accident, she said, swaying slightly in the doorway of the room. —Right after they left.

She must have seen me stiffen.

—They hit a boy with their car. He's dead. A hitchhiker, standing at a bend in the road. They didn't see him the way he was dressed, all in black.

She told me how her boyfriend had walked across the fields for help, how mine had stood on the empty highway, in the dark, the dead body on the gravel at his feet.

I could say nothing. His horror, his guilt, his sorrow were mine.

She left to call her boyfriend back, to ask what exactly the police had said. The boys had been taken home to their families. My boyfriend's parents were separated. His father lived in Europe and I had never met his mother, I wasn't even certain she knew of me. I couldn't bring myself to call. It was after midnight, long past a respectable hour for a telephone to ring. Besides, if he needed me, if he cared at all, surely he would try to get in touch with me.

I lit the blue candle then, put it in the window, and sat on the sill, desperate to speak with him, not able to think, really, only distantly aware of the images flaring in my mind: a tangle of roses on a Calgary hillside, a ridge of chair cutting into my palms. There were others, vague and flitting as dreams, and then, inexplicably, my parents. My father, a bit of a roué, and my mother, a Christian girl of twenty, exactly my age; a real goody-two-shoes, she'd laugh as she told the story. His buddies had teased him to ask her out, and when she'd finally said yes, they'd driven home from their first date in silence, for they had little to talk about. But then his car had hit someone stepping off the trolley. And the way she'd held the wounded man as they'd raced to the hospital, and the way he'd insisted on coming into her house to explain to her father why they'd been so late, well that was how they fell in love.

It came to me, then, as I sat in the window, the candle burning low, that this was that kind of moment, too, the kind that shifts a life. When the flame finally sputtered, extinguishing itself, I knew there was nothing left to do but go to him. I would phone and tell him I was coming. I was sorry to wake his mother, but I had to be there with him.

It was the middle of the night by the time I could get to the apartment where my boyfriend's mother lived. He answered the door, drew me past his mother's bedroom into the living room where he fell into my arms, sobbing. I rocked him gently until the sky began to lighten, then he opened the couch to a bed and I took off my skirt and blouse, and we lay down together, our bodies pressed along their full length, a touch beyond desire, for only love can salve such pain.

—You look like Adam and Eve, his mother said the next morning, never suspecting we were not lovers.

Weeks later, when at last he entered me, I whispered, —I want to have your child. And before a month had passed, he begged, —Marry me. Please.

In defiance of tradition, I wear a suede miniskirt, a translucent white blouse that shows the lace of my brassiere (but no shadow of nipple), and a leopard-skin vest I made myself from the lining of my great-aunt's coat. Nothing could be further, I think, from the satin gown and veil my parents would have wanted. My hair is pulled back from my face, the way he likes it, and pinned with five pink rosebuds, the most we can afford.

The vest is old; the flowers new. The blouse is borrowed, and the candles blue. He slips the ring on my finger: it is old too, a lovely, slender band of white and yellow gold we found in a pawn shop, worn thin by a stranger's hand. We had not intended to marry so soon. At least a year, I told my mother when I showed her my engagement ring, a piece of copper tubing he'd cut and filed smooth. And not, I reassured my girlfriend, until after we came back from Europe.

But I had underestimated the intensity of this love of ours. Every moment apart was agony. We met every weekend in his city or mine, but silly, old-fashioned rules barred us from the women's residence at my university and from the room he rented near his. Only rarely could we afford a hotel room, and so we rubbed against each other in the corners of darkened lobbies, in damp hollows by the river. We grasped at every opportunity that was offered, one night ending up at a rented house where some friends of his lived. We slept on a mattress on the floor, and as we lay there, touching, his friends passed naked through the room and crouched beside us to chat, their penises dangling inches from my eyes though I hid my face in the pillow and pretended to sleep. In the morning, a naked girl outside the bathroom door smirked as I clutched my boyfriend's shirt closer to my chest, and in the kitchen, naked men sipped coffee while I steeped some herbal tea that I hoped would calm the wild eyes of my love who had raved through the night, something wrong with what he'd smoked, he said, gripping my hand.

—I need you, he moaned. —I can't live without you.

—Let's get married now, I offered.

And he answered, —Yes, oh yes.

Outside the church, we double over laughing, relieved it is over, thrilled to have done this thing that is so completely ours. We hug our friends and give them the candles as mementoes of the wedding. They drive us to the outskirts of the city, to the room we've reserved at the Peter Pan Motel.

The room reminds me of summer holidays in the north with my family: the twin double beds with durable spreads and matching curtains, an outdated television hanging from a bracket on the wall. The musty smell has a sobering effect. Coupled now, I feel like my parents: responsible.

—I guess we should call our families, I say.

My new husband goes first. He talks to his mother for a moment, then hands me the telephone.

—I hope you'll be happier than I was, she says.

It is only eight o'clock, too early to go to bed. We kiss a little, but the room is acting on us, making us feel strange.

—Aren't you going to call your parents? he asks.

—In a minute.

I know what they'll think. They'll think I'm pregnant. And it will give me such pleasure to tell them they're wrong. I rehearse the conversation, stalling for time. Nothing has changed, I'll say, except that I'm not going to Europe. We will both stay in school. And we won't start a family until he's established as a sculptor. We have it all planned.

I can't avoid it any longer. I pick up the telephone and dial the numbers slowly, thinking how appropriate the last four digits are: 7734, hell upside down.

My father answers. He must be in the basement: I can hear the thrum of the electric train. No, he says, my mother isn't home.

—I have something to tell you, I say reluctantly, for I had wanted my mother to hear the news first. What you've always said is right, I would have told her. Everything is fine, now that I have a man. —I got married, I blurt out. —Tonight.

—Stupe!

My father's pet name for me explodes in my ear.

—What did you go and do that for? What about university? What about your scholarship?

I lower the receiver to my lap and listen to his voice, the words muffled, but their meaning conveyed in tone and inflection. Gingerly, as though what he is saying has made the plastic volatile, I set the receiver back on its cradle, listening for the click that removes him from my life.

–What did he say?

–Nothing. I don't know. It doesn't matter.

We sit on the edge of the bed, holding hands. My husband has turned on the television. It is a movie, *The Glenn Miller Story*, and the band is playing "In the Mood," my parents' song. I can see them dancing, my mother in her teal-blue dress and her high heels, my father so tall and strong, with his thin airman's moustache and his quiet Jimmy Stewart smile. I feel the sudden urge to call him back, to try to explain, but then June Allyson looks up at Jimmy, and I see my mother, with love in her eyes, lean back in my father's arms, and I know she'll understand even if I say nothing. She'll explain it to him, as she always has, our emissary, our intercessor, this woman who, like the Virgin Mary, always carries a pitcher of oil, not to anoint my father's feet, but to pour on troubled waters.

Everything will be all right, she'll say to him, her voice soothing and kind. Now that our daughter, this difficult, unhappy daughter, finally has a man.

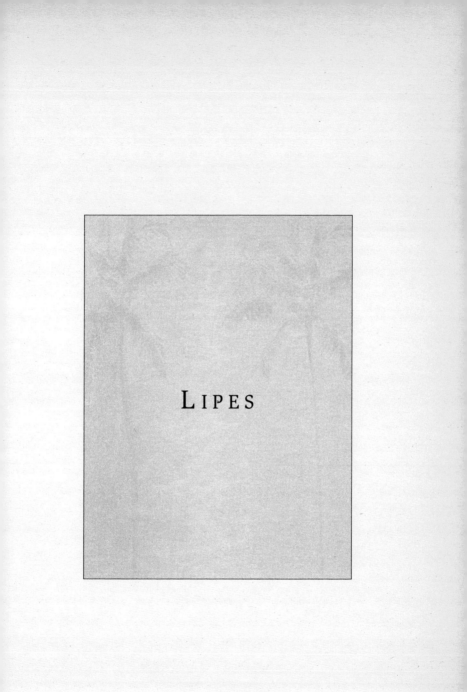

LIPES

Navigating the Kattegat

—ᴎ—

Whatever my eye falls on is foreign, without significance to me. A round wooden coffee table; two narrow couches pushed against each other in the shape of an L; the tall mullioned window that overlooks the harbour. I take pleasure in the thought: Nothing here belongs to me.

Which is not quite true. The suitcase under the couch where I sit has my name on the tag. Inside: one red skirt, one pair of navy-blue pants, three tops, some underwear. Counting all these possessions barely uses the fingers of two hands. There are children's clothes as well, things for the little boy who sleeps at my side, his spun-white curls damp against the woven cover of the couch. I count him too. He is my son.

It took us a year, my husband and me, to reduce ourselves to this. First we sold the car, then the furniture, listing the items in the newspaper: "Leaving the country. Everything must go." My great-aunt's spool bedroom set; the pressback chairs we'd bought for two dollars each; all our wedding gifts, even the pendulum mantel clock from my husband's best friend. We held nothing back. After each piece was carted off, we inked a little higher the red mercury on the savings thermometer we'd cut out of cardboard and tacked to the kitchen wall beside a map of Europe that bristled with coloured stick pins, as if that apartment on the second floor of a house by a river in small-town Ontario were the headquarters for some ambitious, clandestine campaign. What we couldn't sell, we gave away. What we couldn't give away, we threw out.

By most standards, our worldly goods were few. Still, it surprised us how much had accumulated in just three years. By the end of the winter, the red ink had risen to its target, and we'd reduced our belongings to a few boxes of photographs, diaries, books, and artist's tools, which we stored in the basement of my parents' house.

We argued over those boxes. To me, they seemed wrong somehow, a faltering of resolve. I worried that this reserve of effects, however small, might exert some rebounding force, like a moon pulling the tide back to sea. Even the dust lodged in the seams of our shirts might work to draw us home. I remembered the Brazilian mother's voodoo of sprinkling the powdered parings of her fingernails in a departing son's suitcase so he would always feel compelled to return. As a precaution, we sold the luggage our families had given us and bought new travelling bags, new clothes for the trip.

We'll write, we said, but don't expect us back.

From where I sit on the couch, I can see the sliver of cold aquamarine called the Kattegat, a narrow cat's-throat of water that joins the Baltic and North Seas. The plan had been this: my husband, a sculptor, would make art in a studio in the south of France while our young son and I stayed with his father in Sweden. At the end of his three-month scholarship, my husband would join us, and together we'd go to Amsterdam, buy a van, and let it take us where it would.

In our kitchen in Canada, contemplating the map of Europe, on which the mauve lobe of Sweden was a mere hand's breadth from the Mediterranean, we'd congratulated ourselves for tempering our bold adventure with such good sense. In fact, we'd worried a little that we were becoming too much like our parents, lacking in spontaneity, preoccupied with ease. But weeks later, as I rode north through the rain, our two-year-old huddled against my chest and at the wheel, my husband's father, a man I'd just met, my faith in our well-charted course wavered.

It was, of course, a predictable doubt. I do not take decisions easily. I draw up lists of consequences; I prepare charts of pros and cons. I agonize over what is better in the long run, in the short term, for each of us, for the world at large. Once a course is set, I throw myself into making headway, but afterwards I stew, as my mother would say. Perhaps another route would have been better. Perhaps we shouldn't have set out at all. The hard going I am good at. It is the calm at either end that sets me adrift. Even at twenty-three, I know this much.

– Call me Ulrich, my husband's father said, holding my hand to his lips and bowing slightly as my husband introduced

us on a train platform somewhere in central Germany. – Or
Dad, if you prefer.

I could not look back at my husband as the car pulled
away from the station, though I knew he would wave until
we were gone, his hand a pale moth winging the night. I was
afraid that actually seeing him, standing alone in the road,
would make me jump from the car and run back to him. So
instead, I closed my eyes and felt him board his train, felt it
gather speed toward the south, felt the gap between us widen,
what drew us close stretching now, thinning from staunch
cord to string, then a thread, a taut filament, the place where
it fixed to my heart stinging with the strain. When I was
certain that it had no more give to it, that my heart would
surely break, the slender sinew elongated some more, and I
knew then that the bond between us would hold, that there
was no limit to this love.

Ulrich and I drove in silence through the night and all
the next day too. North through Germany, through the
streets of Hamburg and the fields of Schleswig-Holstein,
thick with grazing cows that my son and I made a game of
finding, pointing them out with a chorus of quiet moos;
up the peninsula of Denmark, stopping only for fuel and
briefly to stretch our legs. I watched through the windshield
as spring withdrew, blossom to bud to bare branch. We
caught the night ferry from Frederikshavn, crossed the
Kattegat in the dark, Ulrich speaking German to another
traveller at the ship's rail, me on an orange plastic bench
inside, my son wary and clinging, my arms prickling under
his weight.

The sky lightened as we entered the streets of Göteborg. I rubbed the condensation from the glass and peered through the mist at the stern square buildings rising from the harbour's edge. As we wound up the slope from the water, the buildings pressed closer to the ground and to each other, their façades growing meaner, coarse and haggard, jutting tight against the sidewalks.

– Here we are! Home sweet home, Ulrich announced, pulling up the handbrake and gesturing grandly at a rust-coloured door identical to all the other doors that lined the narrow, empty street.

The apartment is two rooms, no more. I can see it all from where I sit: the galley kitchen and this large bed-sitting room with a desk by the window, table and chairs in the middle, two couches and a coffee table occupying the corner opposite the door. The bathroom is outside, down the hall; it has its own key. When we need to bathe, we heat the water by dropping *kronor* in a gas meter that hangs on the wall above the tub.

A restrained, pared-down existence, this. Perhaps my father-in-law takes comfort in embracing his home with a glance, I think, just as I find joy in carrying all I own in one hand. Everything within reach; little to hamper a sudden urge to depart. But these reduced circumstances may mean something else entirely. Perhaps this is all they can afford. When I first saw the place, I admit my heart sank. Even when my husband and I were students, we had four rooms. How, I wondered, would all of us manage in two?

The woman Ulrich lives with, Ruth, met us at the door. She took my hand, rested her fingers briefly on my son's cheek, then raised her face to Ulrich. I moved past them into the room. Ruth had set the table with sweet buns, marmalade, and plums. There was a red rose in a vase at the centre, cloth napkins with a bright floral pattern at each place. The colour, and the care with which the table had been laid, restored my spirits somewhat. On a stool sat a red plastic truck, almost as big as my son.

— Go on, take it, said Ulrich, his hand at Ruth's waist.
— It's for you, little one. A gift of welcome to Sweden.

But my son clung to my leg, his face in my skirt. Awkwardly, I sat down and he pushed onto my lap, burrowing his head between my breasts. I wrapped my arms around him, stroked his hair, and murmured softly, embracing him with my words, my body's warmth, my scent.

I heard Ulrich sit down heavily on the couch, heard him sigh, — Oh, that feels better.

Out of the corner of my eye I saw Ruth folding his trousers. Against a chair leaned Ulrich's leg. The length of glossy, flesh-coloured plastic made me think of naked dolls. My arms tightened around my son.

— It gets so sore, Ulrich said, as if to apologize, rubbing the stump of his thigh.

I couldn't shift my gaze. His leg, what was left of it, hardly seemed human, the way the skin folded in on itself, fused unnaturally in a seam. I wanted to touch it, feel what happened to bone and blood and muscle when such a vital part was cut away.

—If it's all right, I think I'd like to go outside, I said. —We could use some exercise.

When the door closed behind us, a long, frayed sigh broke from my lips. For two days, I'd been watching my words, my son's every move, watching the features of my father-in-law's face for early warnings that I might be veering from a calm and proper course.

We took a street that appeared to wind toward the water. The sky had cleared. The buildings, which earlier had seemed so squalid, now struck me as almost quaint, venerable rather than decrepit with age. Sailors' cottages or fishermen's flats, perhaps. They shouldered each other congenially, a fraternity of grey brick that parted unexpectedly, delightfully, now and then, to frame a flash of blue.

We rounded a curve, and the street ended abruptly in a sprawling playground. Half a city block had been cleared of buildings and layered with fine white sand contained by logs laid on their sides, tree trunks of such diameter that when my son straddled one, his feet didn't reach the ground. The logs made me feel at home. Although the sun hadn't yet topped the tenements, mothers with children were congregating on the wooden benches that hedged the giant sandbox, claiming their territory with strollers heaped with pails, shovels, and assorted vehicles in plastic shades of red, yellow, and blue.

—Truck! my son cried out, pointing at the toys.

I knelt and hugged him tightly. —We'll bring your truck here to play. We'll be fine. You'll see. Everything will be okay.

By the time we returned from our walk, Ulrich and Ruth
were in bed, wound around each other on the couch nearest
the door.

—We'll all have a nap, now? Ulrich said, a slight Swedish
inflection lifting the tail of his sentences. —We'll catch up
from our trip, then we'll show you the town.

It had not been discussed, but the sleeping arrangement
was obvious. My son and I were to share the second couch.
I took off his clothes and tucked him between the covers.
Then, hesitating just a moment, I pulled off my own pants
and shirt, conscious of my breasts, still large from nursing,
and my body, naked to carefully averted eyes.

Although my son and I have been here only three days, we
have already settled into certain habits. Ulrich rises early to
go to work at the bearing factory; Ruth and I share coffee
before she leaves for the cancer laboratory.

Despite her age, Ruth seems almost childlike to me, her
voice trilling one-word sentences, filling the voids in our conversation with eager smiles and offers of things to eat, things
to look at, pamphlets that describe places we might like to
visit. She and I are tentative with each other. I have noticed
how she quickly finds something else to do when Ulrich turns
his attention to me. But she has formed a bond with my son.
The first day she bought him a sailor's hat, which he puts on
the minute he awakens. He sits and listens wide-eyed to her
stories, mesmerized, as am I, by her lilting tones, though not
understanding a word of what she says. When I first heard the

language on the ferry, I thought of the soft mewling of cats, enquiring but insistent, insinuating.

My son and I pass the mornings in the park with the other children and the mothers who smile and speak to me in Swedish, my boy is that blond. I experiment with the phrases Ulrich has been teaching me: *Hur står det till?* How are you? *Sådant fint väder!* What fine weather! And most important, *Så tråkigt, jag förstår inte.* I'm so sorry, but I don't understand.

At noon, Ulrich always telephones to ask if we are happy, if there is anything we need. Later, while my son naps, I find things to do in the kitchen, which is the only way I can think of to help. The first day, I made mudpies: chocolate cookies that don't need to be cooked. There is no stove in the tiny galley, only a two-burner hotplate and, since there were no cooking utensils in the drawers, I had to estimate the proportions. That night, Ruth showed me the fold-out tin oven. She mixed dollops of sugar and flour, butter, eggs, and cinnamon together to bake a *fantasie küchen*. The next day, I found a shop that sold measuring cups and spoons, then I, too, set up the oven over the gas burners and baked an apple pie. Today I bought yeast for bread.

Every day, Ulrich returns to the apartment promptly at four, two hours before Ruth arrives home. He is a man not of habit so much as ritual. At predictable interludes, when he has his morning coffee, at his homecoming each afternoon, in the hour of silence when he reads at night, he gives himself over to the moment, treasures it as if it were his most favoured companion.

I've taken careful note of what pleases my husband's father, and now when his key turns in the lock, the Earl Grey is steeping, and the things I have baked are arranged beautifully on the coffee table in front of his couch. This afternoon, I laid uniform slices of warm bread on a pretty blue plate I found on the top shelf, spooned plum preserves, his favourite, into a fluted china dish, and set square pats of butter on ice chips in a cut-glass bowl. (Though I am secretly proud of my resourcefulness, I don't tell him how I searched the apartment in vain for a hammer and finally, wrapping the ice in a plastic shopping bag, I whacked it to bits with my boot.) His exclamations of pleasure are gratifying, but I do this for myself, too. The silky feel of flour on my fingertips and the smell of swelling yeast remind me of my mother, of my own new family, and I feel a little less alone.

As we sip our afternoon tea, Ulrich tells me stories. How at the beginning of the war he'd married his childhood sweetheart and immediately after their honeymoon, he'd been sent to the front, so the marriage was never consummated (– She was frigid that first time, he said. – Who could know there'd never be another?). How he'd become a sapper, a defuser of bombs, a reluctant soldier devoted not to Hitler but to the chemistry of explosion, and how once out of frustration he'd kicked what he thought was a dud, and it blasted off half his foot. He'd climbed out the hospital window to visit his girlfriend (– I never was one to sit still for long, he laughed) and, without proper care, the wound had become infected, and first his foot, then his shin, and finally most of his leg had been amputated. He lay in hospital for months, then, glad to be out of the war but not at peace, for he was a man who had one leg and two women, a frigid wife whom he loved, and the woman who carried his child. (I'd heard this part of the story before, though he gave no hint of the pregnant woman's pity, or her fear.)

The rest I knew by heart. She bore him two more sons before he became their legal father. In the years of hardship that followed the war, they got by on what he earned as an interpreter for American soldiers until, lured by the stories of a Red Cross nurse, he took the family to Canada, then back to Germany, and to Canada again, criss-crossing the Atlantic, back and forth between two countries, abandoning each in turn to satisfy his yearning for the other. Finally, my husband, his brothers, and his mother returned to Canada, where they waited for Ulrich to join them, waited for years, his mother sending borrowed money for her husband's passage, but still he didn't come; all of them, except my husband, giving up at last.

– Canada is my country. I love it more than the place I was born, Ulrich said as he stared beyond me to the Kattegat.

He didn't ask for understanding or forgiveness, only that I hear him out.

– I couldn't go back to her. There was too much bitterness. So I stayed behind. I gave the country of my heart to my sons.

Ulrich hardly seems like my husband's father or the grandfather of my son. They both look distinctly German, stalwart and blond, while Ulrich could be Irish, he's that short and dark, with mischievous, squinting eyes and a sly, closed-up smile, as if he's seen the gold at the end of the rainbow and might tell you about it too, if only you'd think to ask.

This afternoon, while we drank our tea, he told the Swedish part of his story. How he was driving the German autobahn on a clear summer's day when he saw two girls hitchhiking by the side of the road. They were on their way to Göteborg, they said. He offered to drive them and brought the girls to this apartment door.

—You've met Ruth, their mother, he said.

She was German too, had come to Sweden when her girls were babies, at the beginning of the war. Her husband, a doctor, had stayed in Berlin. Near the end, in the chaos, operating without gloves, he'd cut his hand, which became infected. He'd lost his mind, part of his brain too, removed in a lobotomy, though he is still alive, a man-child, somewhere in eastern Europe, while Ruth remains in Sweden, her girls now grown.

—You can understand, Ulrich said, why I stayed.

I had never known lovers of such an age. Ulrich and Ruth have children who have children of their own, and yet they kiss like teenagers when they part and when they meet again. Not a routine peck on the lips like the one my father gives my mother every night after work, but long, lingering kisses, full on the lips, ending with shy murmurs of pleasure as if they share some sweet aftertaste. I've grown accustomed to the cramped quarters, the lack of privacy, even to the rank havarti cheese and blood sausage Ulrich adores, but I can't get used to this. I turn away from their intimacies. Such public display strikes me as unseemly in people so old. And it stirs in me longings for my husband that I dare not think about.

Sitting on the couch, my son asleep at my side, I allow myself to feel the longing now, feel the sinew thickening, drawing back into itself, that strain again in the vicinity of my heart, not an emptying now, a filling up.

When my husband telephoned an hour ago, I became suddenly still at the sound of his voice.

–What's wrong? I asked.

We had so little money, we had agreed not to call.

–I'm here in Göteborg.

–My god. What happened? I said.

What awful thing could have forced him to leave the art colony after only three days?

–I missed you, he whispered.

He could not bear for us to be apart. Now I realize, neither could I.

Ulrich and Ruth have gone to the airport to pick him up. I walk to the window to watch for their return, but it is night and all I see is my own reflection in the glass, a long, solemn face, unruly curls pulled firmly back. The window is very tall. I have to stand on a chair to reach the latch. When I open it, the air against my cheeks is ripe with ocean. I lean far out, hoping to catch a first glimpse of Ulrich's car, but the street below stays resolutely empty. I look out toward the Kattegat. A ferry moves into the harbour, its form traced in lights. The night is so black that sky and water are one. The boat seems to hover, adrift in the dark.

We'll make a new plan, I think. We'll take the ferry to Frederikshavn. Then the train to Amsterdam. We can leave in a week. Maybe two. We can be in Greece by August instead of October; Israel by the fall. My mind accelerates, calculating what my husband's unexpected return will mean, to our itinerary, to our budget, to our stay in Göteborg. After all, the apartment has barely contained the four of us; how will it accommodate one more?

—Water of life! Ulrich exclaims as he pours each of us a shot of *akvavit* into miniature crystal goblets.

He raises his glass in a toast. —To my son, my new daughter, my grandson, he says. —To this reunion and many more.

Lined up on the couch, we sip at the clear liquor, exclaiming at its fire and its subtle, perfume taste, like strangers making small talk at a party. I long to be alone with my husband, do more than touch the back of his hand.

Ulrich drains his glass in one swallow.

—I was going to save this for later but, well, why wait, now that you are here?

He pauses, as if to allow us to make an argument.

—You see, I knew you meant to travel once you came back to Sweden. I thought it would be three months from now, of course, and I'd have time, but here you are, I'll give it to you now.

Ulrich looks at Ruth and they both beam at us.

What on earth is he talking about? I think.

Ulrich laughs. – A vehicle! I've bought you a car!

The baby stirs. Ulrich has all but shouted, he's so pleased with himself. I squeeze my husband's hand and go to our son, kneeling by his makeshift bed on the floor to pat his bum so he'll slip back into sleep. I look across at my husband. He is staring into his glass as if the future were charted there.

– But we're going to Amsterdam, he says after a while. – To buy a van.

– I know, I know. Ulrich brushes his son's words aside with a little wave as he reaches for the bottle of *akvavit*. – But this little Saab, wait till you see her! You'll love her. After we're finished, she'll run like a kitten. And I'll show you how to take care of her on the road, how to change the spark plugs, everything. I know you can't sleep in such a little car, but I've thought of that too. You can borrow my camping gear. What an adventure you'll have! How I envy you, you and your little family, wandering through Europe in your little Swedish car.

Ulrich, transported by his vision, seems not to notice that everyone has fallen silent except the baby, whose fussing is quickly escalating. I leave the room to walk with him up and down the hall outside. When I finally return, my son asleep on my shoulder, the apartment is dark. Everyone is in bed. I lay the child on his mattress of pillows by the desk, but he whimpers and clings to me, so I lie down at his side.

I must have fallen asleep too, for the sky is already beginning to lighten when next I open my eyes. The Kattegat is visible again, a grey-blue wash at the horizon. I rise and go to my husband, who is huddled deep in the covers, his back to the room.

Ulrich convinces us to look at the car, at least. We can't refuse, although our disinclination to see things his way hardens as we pull up beside the vehicle marooned in a deserted parking lot. It is a humpbacked little car, pale blue. We cannot be vagabonds in a baby-blue sedan. We can't pull off the road and park under the willows to sleep. It is all wrong. The Saab simply won't do.

We circle the car in silence, thinking not of its merits but of how to refuse Ulrich's gift.

—No, my husband says finally, flatly. —We don't want this car.

—Now don't be too hasty, son.

Ulrich pats my husband's arm. —I know it isn't exactly what you had in mind. It needs a little work, sure, but you don't have to leave right away. We'll fix it together, father and son. Here, get in and drive it around a bit. You'll see. It'll do the trick.

Ulrich dangles the car keys so close in front of my husband's nose that, for a minute, I'm afraid he'll take them in his mouth and spit them back in his father's face.

—No. I don't need to drive it. Aren't you listening to me? We don't want it. We're going to buy a van. In Amsterdam. Just like we planned.

—Where? Where, exactly, will you buy this van?

Ulrich has dropped his lilting Swedish tones. His voice has deepened, become guttural. —What makes you think there are vans in Amsterdam? Is this some hippie story you've heard, from one of your long-haired friends?

He had opened the hood of the car to demonstrate some feature of the engine. He slams it shut.

—Ask *me*, why don't you? I've been to Amsterdam more times than you can shake a stick at. No one has ever tried to sell me a van.

His voice softens again.

—Here is a car, right here, a perfectly good little car. Bought and paid for. Take it. Please.

My husband's eyes never leave the asphalt. I think he might be tempted by his father's pleading.

—Take it! Ulrich shouts, pounding his fist on the fender, making the car shiver.

I recall the stories my husband has told me. How his father would line up his sons and beat them one by one to find out which of them had lied, or cheated, or stolen, or started the fight, my husband getting the brunt of it, always, because he smiled. It has been like this as long as he can remember: when he is nervous, his face cracks with a foolish grin. He is grinning now. It makes his father furious. It fills me with fear.

My son draws closer to me, gripping my skirt. I pick him up and wander away from the men, rubbing his back, comforting myself too, with the rhythm of the stroking. No voice in my childhood was ever raised in anger. Sharp sarcastic words, taut silences, yes, but though there was often the tension of a gathering storm, if it erupted, it wreaked its havoc elsewhere. Behind us, Ulrich's words lash at his son.

– Bought and paid for. Do you understand? Paid for in cash.

I'd have given in, made do somehow, even if meant mouthing false gratitude, then sold the car once we reached the Netherlands.

– Maybe we should consider it, I suggest later, as we sit on the park bench, watching our son play in the sand. – If he's already paid for it . . .

– That's his problem. He should have asked us first.

I have seen my husband weep for the birthdays and Christmases that passed unremarked by his father, who lived an ocean away and would have drifted out of sight forever but for my husband, the youngest son, who pursued him and made fast a connection his father would have let slip. In a family of soldiers, mathematicians, and clerks, my husband and his father have always stood apart, the artist and the wanderer, bound by rules of their own. Ulrich, alone among all the members of our families, encouraged our journey, which was why my husband insisted we set out from Göteborg, from his father's doorstep.

Now he can't wait to leave.

– Look, he's known for ages you were coming, and bringing our son. Did he really expect you to sleep in the same room with him and Ruth for three months? And now he wants all of us to stay here while he fixes up that wreck of a car. How can he possibly believe we can live in that little apartment, all five of us? My mother was right. He never thinks about anybody but himself. I don't know why I expected that with me, with us, he'd be any different.

We linger at the park until dusk. When we return, the door opposite their apartment is open, and Ulrich is limping down the hall toward us, carrying a large wooden box.

—We rent that room for storage, he explains, setting down the box and wiping the sweat from his forehead. — We're clearing it out for you. Now you can stay as long as you want.

He pauses, rubbing his thigh. Through the fabric of his trousers I can see the ridge where the artificial leg joins the stump.

—Until you leave for Amsterdam, of course, he adds.

The car is never mentioned, not now or in the days that follow. We have no idea what has happened to it, if it still sits in the centre of that parking lot. We don't ask. The Saab becomes just another rocky shoal in the difficult relations between my husband and his father.

Cleaning out the storage room, my husband finds a wooden toilet-seat cover that, for the next several days, he carries to the park and, while I build sand cities with our son, he sits on the bench and carves the wood, gouging long, fragrant curls that mound at his feet. As I smooth the sand for my son's highways, I watch my husband, silently willing him to lift his head, to look at me, but his eyes never leave the madonna and child taking shape in the wood. I don't mind, really. I love to see him so absorbed. I look with satisfaction from father to son, one pushing a knife through wood, the other a truck through sand, both with their brows furrowed in concentration, each with his tongue poking out from the left side of his mouth, oblivious to his surroundings, no hint of pain or pleasure visible in either face.

We bide our time, waiting for the right moment to depart. We talk of nothing but our trip, the countries we intend to visit, the museums and galleries we plan to see. Ulrich throws himself into our project. He hands over his language books, though he keeps the one on Finnish grammar for himself. In spare moments he is adding this to the half-dozen European languages he speaks with a fluency that astonishes me.

Every night he brings home gifts from his lunch-hour forages at the Salvation Army store: sturdy oiled-canvas coats with zippered fleece linings, army-surplus sleeping bags, single-lens reflex cameras for both of us, a stroller for our son, a length of deerskin that he cuts and sews into money pouches for us to wear under our shirts.

–You need so much! he exclaims, pressing on us a hard-cover book describing the capitals of Europe, and a military map case with rows of pockets on one side, and on the other, a clear plastic compartment that he has stuffed with road maps of every country we've named.

–We have to get out of here while we can still walk, my husband mumbles under his breath as Ruth and Ulrich collect the tea things from the kitchen. He kicks the red truck away from his chair. –As it is, we'll have to leave most of this stuff behind.

A week passes. Ulrich and Ruth have been thinking of

moving, even they find the apartment too small, and a friend has told them of a house the right size, in a good neighbourhood, at a manageable price. Ulrich insists we come along when they go to look at it.

—You're family, and this is a big decision for us, he says, putting his arm around his son's shoulders. — I want your approval.

The house is in a suburb, far away from the Kattegat. It is small and plain, but I have come to expect a certain functionality in the architecture of this country. The Swedes, to me, seem practical and subdued, not given to wanton expression, except in their bedrooms, if their reputation is to be believed, but certainly not in the embellishment of their houses, where design is disciplined, even straitlaced. Only in the cadences of their speech do I detect a trace of whimsy.

The yard behind the house is enclosed by a tall, small-leafed hedge. At the back, the lawn is displaced by a rise of grey stone.

—Oh, it reminds me of Canada, says Ulrich, turning to us eagerly, his eyes glazed with desire. —Don't you think so?

He insists on posing us on the rock for photographs, each of us alone and then in combination. The baby and me; my husband and me; the baby and my husband. — I'll make a darkroom in the basement. I'll send you prints, big blow-ups: the first day at our new home!

Exhilarated by possibility, Ulrich paces the yard, then the house. Inside, he elaborates his grand idea. Each room will have a theme. The kitchen, a ship's galley; the bathroom, all in cedar like a sauna.

— And this, he says, striding into the largest of two small bedrooms and taking Ruth in his arms. —This will be Arabian Nights. What do you think, *Schätzlein*? We'll drape gauze from the ceiling and over the windows, the colour of amber and lapis lazuli. That's right, isn't it? Or am I getting sultans and pharaohs all mixed up? Never mind. We won't have a mattress. Only pillows. I'll sew them, enormous silk pillows, with tassels. And you'll dance for me, the dance of the seven veils, eh?

And, like the King of Siam, he waltzes Ruth around the plain little room with one small window that overlooks the drab Swedish street with its rows of small windows looking out from rooms, each one identical, I suspect, to this.

We agree to stay until Ulrich and Ruth take possession of the house on the first of July, exactly one month's time. My husband will help with the move. It is decided. Setting the date is a relief to me. We are finally underway again. But my husband grows more irritable, even though the new house distracts his father from our plans. Now, Ulrich's daily rummagings at the Salvation Army yield not travel gear, but swaths of drapery fabric, odd lamps, and a sundial, slightly bent but still functional, for his new backyard.

My husband abandons the madonna and child.

— I can't be expected to do bas-relief on a toilet seat, for Christ's sake.

I suggest he do some sketching. Göteborg, for instance, or the Swedish landscape.

–But this place looks just like Canada, he grumbles. –The buildings are all so ugly and grey.

And so, when Ulrich suggests a Sunday excursion to Slottskogen, the celebrated park at the centre of the city, I respond with enthusiasm. Ruth has shown us pictures. There is a zoo, botanical gardens, a lake with pink flamingoes and snowy egrets.

– It'll be lovely. We can wade in the water, and you can draw! Surely you'll find something there to inspire you.

It is only the second week of June, but the weather has turned suddenly warm. The paths through the park are swarming with families pushing strollers, children weaving in and out, trailing batons of cotton candy. Young lovers lounge on the grass, leaning close to conceal their intimacies. Everyone has loosened their clothes, slowed their pace in the unexpected heat. Strangers smile at each other, remarking on the fine day. Our son toddles across the grass, and when he stumbles and falls, a young man whisks him upright and plays a finger game with him to make him laugh. At the lake, I lift him up to the fence and point out the exotic birds perched precariously on one leg.

–I feel right at home, Ulrich says with a laugh.

We've brought a basket of food, some books, a transistor radio. Ulrich and Ruth find an unclaimed patch of grass and spread their blanket.

– It's like a goddamn suburb, my husband complains, leaning against a tree a few yards away.

Ruth is setting out the food. I should help, but first I feel compelled to try to alleviate my husband's mood.

– Isn't it wonderful, the people all coming outside like this on a Sunday? It feels like a holiday. Look how happy everyone is!

My exclamations only seem to irritate him more. I wait for some sign, some hint of what I might do to make him smile at me, but he sits silent, his chin in his hands, staring at the families picnicking on the grass around us. I can't think of anything else to say, and so I kiss his forehead and go to Ulrich, who is playing with his grandson, pushing Dinky cars along the blanket's stripes.

My husband joins us when we eat, though he barely says a word. After lunch, we set our empty plates on the grass and settle down to read and doze. Ulrich and Ruth lie close together, holding hands, their eyes closed. The passing hours have nudged the shade from our blanket and I revel in the heat, hiking up my skirt to feel the sun on my thighs.

Our son begins to whimper. My husband shoves a toy at him, an inflatable book with pictures of trucks and cars and boats, but he tosses it back to the blanket. He thrusts his arms toward me and whines to be picked up. His cheeks are flushed. Perhaps he has a fever, I think, and reach for him, but I am not fast enough. My husband scoops him up and shakes him, shakes him hard, until our little boy's head flops side to side, stifling his whine.

I grab the child from my husband's arms, both of us, my son and I, suddenly stiff and wide-eyed, me softening first, hushing him, rocking slowly on my heels, back and forth, back and forth, holding him to me.

– We're leaving, my husband says, gathering up our things. – We have a baby, you know. We can't stay all day in the sun.

He heaps toys, books, juice bottle in the stroller.

– Come on, he says to me, that foolish smile on his face.

Ulrich and Ruth, dozy from the food and the heat, take some time to realize what is happening. They sit up, but we are already walking away from them, across the grass, though not yet out of earshot when Ulrich says, – I don't understand it. That boy is so bourgeois.

The next morning, while Ulrich and Ruth are at work, we pack our things. My husband has decided it is time to leave. We make excuses to each other: if we wait to help with the move, school will be out and the trains filled with holiday-makers; Amsterdam will be crowded; it will be harder than ever to buy a van. But the truth came out as we talked through the night.

– Face it, my husband said when I argued for one last try. – My father and I just can't get along.

In the afternoon, we find a shop that sells barbecues, and we buy a red one for Ulrich, a combination housewarming, Father's Day, and thank-you gift.

– Though why we should give him anything, I don't know, my husband says.

We tell Ulrich our change of plans when he telephones at noon. He hardly responds, as if he's expected this all along.

When he returns from work, our suitcases are at the door. I have made an early dinner: boiled cabbage and fried blood sausage, caraway-seed potatoes. When Ruth arrives, we eat in silence and afterwards we give Ulrich his gift. Our train is scheduled to depart in less than an hour, but even so, we can hardly find enough to say.

Ruth kisses us goodbye at the apartment door. There's not room for all of us in the car, even though we are leaving behind most of what Ulrich has given us. At the station, my husband hurries ahead to buy our tickets. The train is delayed. We find a bench near the platform and sit down to wait, our two suitcases at our feet.

– Several years ago, Ulrich begins, when I was travelling by train from Sweden to Germany, I met a young fellow from America.

I am sitting between my husband and his father. My husband stares down the track, looking away from us. I take his hand in mine, gently draw him closer. I rest my other hand on Ulrich's arm. If only I can be soft enough, make some quiet, healing gesture, say exactly the right thing, I might solder this rift.

– Yes? I say to Ulrich, encouraging him to go on.

– The young man had no money. He had no ticket either. He had sneaked onto the train and had managed to avoid the conductor at every stop by hiding in the toilet or moving between the cars.

– He was a very interesting young man. You'd have liked him. He had travelled all over the world, doing odd jobs here and there, hopping trains, sleeping in haystacks, you name it.

I very much admired him, I can tell you. I'm too old for that now, but if there hadn't been a war, I would have done what he was doing when I was young, I would.

– We talked and laughed. He had such a nice laugh, loud but natural, as if he would rather be laughing than anything else in the world. The type of laugh you rarely hear, come to think of it. I shared my sandwiches with him, I invited him to come to Sweden. It was very pleasant, passing the time with this young man. Actually, we lost all track of time. Suddenly, there were men in uniform coming down the aisle. We were at the border of Germany and officials had boarded the train to check our passports.

– The young man was trapped. A border guard was stationed at each end of the car; the officials were moving in our direction.

Ulrich laughs a little, remembering the scene, but it is a bitter laugh. At the sound, my husband raises his head but he says nothing, still refuses to look at us.

– We Germans learned a long time ago the art of being thorough and efficient, Ulrich continues. Anyway, I pulled out my wallet, took out all the money I had. I was sure it would be enough for him to pay for his ticket. I tried to give it to him, but he shook his head and pushed it away.

– The officials were at our side by now. They asked for our passports and our tickets, which we gave them, all except the young man, of course. '*Amerikanisch?*' they said to him. He nodded. When they asked for his ticket, he just shrugged. I thought I could help, being German myself, and so I started to explain that he was a foreigner and didn't understand our system and had thought he could purchase a ticket on the train. I showed them the money, saying I would pay for him. But the young man jumped up before I could finish, bumping into me so hard I dropped the money. It scattered over the floor. Then he held out his hands to the officials as if for handcuffs. 'I don't have a friggin' ticket,' he said. 'Take me away.'

Ulrich imitates the young man's accent with eerie accuracy. His tongue is chameleon, switching so convincingly from German to Swedish, and now to a southern drawl, that I can easily imagine him, a handsome young Bavarian leaning on his crutches, interpreting for the American soldiers who took over his town, earning a dollar however he could to feed the little boys who lined up with their mother for rations of powdered milk and flour. Picking up the soldiers' inflection, hoarding it all these years, not knowing how he'd use it, but, like those scavenged lamps and books, hanging on to it just the same.

– They marched the young American lad off the train then, Ulrich is saying. Distracted by his voice, I've missed some of the story, but nothing critical, it seems.

– I looked out as they passed on the platform. I wanted to do something, you understand, make some small gesture of sympathy, or support. Just when they were beside our window, the young man looked up and saw me. He grinned. I smiled back. I felt so sorry for him.

Ulrich pauses, as though he is still wondering what he might have done to make the story come out differently. I wish he would finish. I want to say something, anything, that will make my husband and his father look at each other, at least shake hands, but our train is already pulling into the station, and my husband is standing now, picking up the suitcases. I rise, too, and lift our son.

—Don't be in such a rush, Ulrich says. —The train won't leave for a few minutes yet. Do you know what that young man did? He gave me the finger. Then he lifted his arm the rest of the way and made the Nazi salute. To me, of all people. I was horrified. I fell back in my seat. Even from inside that train, I could hear him. He laughed and laughed, as if it were some huge joke.

We are crossing the platform, my husband striding toward the train, widening the gap between him and the rest of us. Ulrich walks beside me, his hand on my arm, but I cannot keep in step with him: he walks too slowly, and his gait is irregular, from his artificial leg, I suppose. His mouth is open slightly, as if he intends the story to go on but can't remember what comes next.

My husband is showing our tickets to the conductor. He lifts his foot to the first step to the railway car, then seems to change his mind and instead stands beside the conductor to wait for us to catch up.

—Well, goodbye then, he says curtly to his father.

Ulrich puts his hands on his son's shoulders and bends forward in that European way, lightly brushing his cheek against one side of his son's face, then the other. My husband accepts his father's gesture, but his body remains taut. Their eyes never meet. If any words pass between them, they are too hushed for me to hear.

My husband climbs the steps and, without looking back, turns down the aisle. Ulrich lifts his grandson from my arms, blows loud kisses against the little boy's belly until he laughs with delight.

I can see my husband in a window now, halfway down the car, beckoning.

— We have to leave now, I say to Ulrich.

— But I've always been the one to leave, he says softly, leaning down to kiss my cheek.

I take back my son. I kiss Ulrich quickly and turn toward the train. My husband at the window, my son against my breast, this man I am leaving, alone on the platform. My heart tugs so, in every direction, I am surprised I can take a step.

THE DISTANCE TO DELPHI

—◊—

It didn't take us long to recover from our arrival at the village of Rhodini.

We had left Athens early one morning, driving past the port of Piraeus with its jostle of fishing boats and grey battleships hulking beneath the Stars and Stripes. We were headed for Patras, on the far end of Peloponnesus, where we'd heard we could catch a ferry to Italy.

—Let's visit Delphi on the way, I suggested to my husband. —After all, it's the centre of the earth.

I knew better, of course, but the myth I'd read in school appealed to me: Zeus releasing two eagles, one from the east and one from the west, ordering them to fly toward each other, then when they met at Delphi, marking the spot with a stone, the *omphalos*, navel of the earth. The ancient Greeks built a temple around that sacred stone. I hadn't forgotten the words they'd carved on its portal: Know Thyself. This was the mantra of Apollo, Zeus's favourite son and brother to Dionysus, whose dark ecstasies Apollo countered with perfect logic. In the Greek pantheon, I liked Apollo best: god of the sun, law-giver and prophet, absolver of guilt, restorer of moral order to the body and the soul. Know thyself, he said. I'd first heard these words from my mother, a Presbyterian born on the other side of the world. Now that I was so close to their source I wanted to see them for myself.

My husband drove the van, which we'd bought in Amsterdam, driving steadily south through Europe as the summer cooled. Our son played on the piece of foam we'd laid in the back as a mattress. I was the navigator, a role of limited consequence since my husband chose the route and did not easily accommodate a change of plan.

We would skirt the south shore of mainland Greece, he determined, stop at the oracle, and cross to the peninsula of Peloponnesus near its western edge. Too late, I saw our mistake. What he'd taken for a road was only an elevation line on the map. To get to Delphi, we should have headed north then cut through the hills down to Mount Parnassos. With my finger, I traced our route back to Athens, to the way we should have gone. We'd already travelled an hour, maybe two, out of our way.

– No, it's too far. We can't go back, my husband said when I showed him our error and how we might correct it. – Besides, we've seen enough ruins.

The highway we were on continued south across the

Isthmus of Corinth. Except for this connecting strip of land, Peloponnesus would be just another Greek island in the Aegean. Instead, it dangles from the mainland like a swollen tongue all but cut off at the root.

We turned west, onto a road that followed the north shore of the peninsula, manoeuvring between the water of the Gulf of Corinth and hills that rose sharply on our left. Clusters of white stuccoed houses were imbedded here and there in the barren slopes. As the shadows lengthened, we looked for a blind of trees, some deserted village street, or an empty stretch of beach where we could pull off the road to sleep. Night fell. I settled our little boy into bed in the back of the van. Still we drove, finding not so much as a widening of gravel at the shoulder. I was steeling myself to the prospect of driving through the night when I spotted a crescent of pebbled sand, luminous in the moonlight.

– There. Isn't that a lane?

We veered down the rocky gully to a curve of vacant shore, where we stared for several moments at the waves. We couldn't tell if they were advancing with the tide. Afraid of waking up to find ourselves immersed, we parked some distance from the water, then we closed the red-chequered curtains and crawled onto the mattress, one of us on either side of our sleeping son.

In the morning I saw that we had driven down a dry stream bed. A village squatted at the far end of the sickle beach. As I stepped out of the van, a boy with curly black hair seemed to walk out of the sunrise, leading two donkeys with baskets strapped to their backs. I cupped my hand and lifted it to my mouth, pantomiming drinking, feeling a little foolish. He shook his head slowly, unsmiling, and continued on his way, but when he returned a short time later without the donkeys, he motioned to us to follow him into the village, into an olive grove where a cement well rose out of the hard-packed earth. We filled our plastic containers from a bucket that we hauled up on ropes. When I bent to pick up two jugs, the boy took them from me, hoisting one on each skinny shoulder. There was nothing else for me to do. I took my son's hand and followed my husband and the village boy back to the van.

— *Efharisto*, I said, when we arrived back at our beach.

He admitted the smallest of smiles. Encouraged, I motioned for him to wait, and while my husband stowed the water jugs, I rummaged in the back of the van, returning with three coins: a quarter, a nickel, and a dime. I offered the money to the boy, holding out my hand to him and smiling, hoping he would understand that I meant it not as payment but as a keepsake, a token.

— Canada, I explained, adding the only other Greek word I knew. — *Parakalo*. Please.

He picked up the quarter and turned it over, examining the caribou. He weighed its heft, then he pitched it into the back of the van. I listened for meaning in the tumble of words that fell from his hard little mouth. I had offended him. But how? Should I not have offered money? Or did he want *drachmae* instead?

There was nothing to be done. He was already gone, his heels leaving impressions like hoofprints in the coarse sand.

We were alone at our end of the beach. The few villagers who passed by to tend vineyards farther down the shore nodded briefly. We decided to stay for a few days, parking the van under a tall thatch of bamboo at the edge of the sand.

The next morning, the boy who had shown us the well brought a man to our little camp. He was large, built solid as a wrestler on a Greek vase, but he was old, his hair grizzled and the skin on his hands well-worn. He introduced himself as Pappos.

I knew from a childhood friend that the word meant grandfather, so I pointed to the man, then to the boy. — Pappos? I asked.

The old man shook his head and spread wide his arms to embrace the village in the distance. — Pappos!

The village was called Rhodini and he was, it seemed, the patriarch. He insisted we call him Pappos too, and when we nodded in agreement, he produced from his pants' pocket a bottle of wine, which he handed to me with a flourish.

I thanked him as best I could. He spoke no English and I, no Greek, but something in his manner reassured me he understood.

— *Thempirazi*, the old man said, waving aside my concerns when I tried to apologize for the coins I'd offered the boy. — *Thempirazi*.

I didn't know what it meant, but the word cancelled everything, wiped the sand smooth.

It has only been a week, but already, every morning, our son watches for Pappos, who saunters down the beach, his hands deep in the pockets of his baggy green pants. While our little boy runs to meet his new friend, my husband and I wait in the shade of the van, as we have learned to do. Pappos jiggles his hands in his pockets. My son must choose. He points to one side of the old man's trousers and Pappos draws out a small pepper, passes it to the boy, then dips his hand in again to retrieve a large white onion. Our son looks disappointed. He is only two, but he plays the game well. He sticks out his lower lip in a pout. Pappos laughs and digs into his other pocket. Slowly, straight-faced, the old man slides out a bottle of *portokali*. The little boy smiles. He trades the vegetables for the sweet orange drink and, hand in hand, they walk the rest of the way to the van.

    – *Kalimera*, the old man says to us.

    – *Kalimera*, we reply. Good morning.

    Pappos gives us the pepper and the onion. One day, it is a bottle of freshly pressed olive oil; another, a bunch of grapes and a handful of limes. We accept his gifts without protest or exchange. We have nothing the old man wants. He never lingers. He seems only to be checking that we are still here and safe, the way a kind father checks his children's beds at night.

He touches our little boy's sun-whitened hair, his blue eyes.

– *Galanos*, he says softly to himself, then he bows to us and walks back along the beach the way he came, his shadow in the early-morning light trailing long and thin behind him.

I touch my son's eyes, too. – *Galanos*, I say.

I think it must be a blessing, or a charm for good luck.

It means simply, blue.

In the heat of the day, a fisherman from the village stops at our beach. His name is Xaralambos; he is teaching me to speak. We sit cross-legged in the shade and he points to the blue shirt he wears, to my son's blue eyes, to the azure water of the bay.

– *Galanos*, he says.

Sometimes, we draw pictures in the sand.

– Hills, I say, pointing first to my drawing, then to the mainland across the water where Mount Parnassos shelters the marble temple of Delphi, which I cannot see but which I imagine, white and serene within its mantle of oaks. The centre of the earth, the soul of ancient Greece.

Xaralambos mimics my movements with his stick: the drawing, the distant hills. Then he says a word that sounds to me like "Christmas."

I search the horizon for a clue to the meaning of what he has said. Finding nothing there, I search within the word itself, for I often find remnants of my language in his. The drawing in the sand, for instance. *Graphicos.* Graph. Graphic. Geography.

Christmas. Christen. Eucharist. Charisma. I stare at the hills, but his word eludes me. — Christmas, I say.

Xaralambos shakes his head. He sounds out the word one syllable at a time, contorting his thin lips. I could love this man, his willingness to make me speak. I lift my tongue tight to my palate and speak from far back in my throat, finding a sound from my Scottish great-great-grandmother, some-thing in the way she might say loch, that approximates his *xi*.

— *Xrismos*, I say.

Correcting myself, I shift the inflection to the end. If I can pronounce it perfectly, I think, its meaning will come clear. I try again. — *Xrismos*.

— *Endaksi!* Xaralambos grins.

When he smiles, which is often, he shows a jumble of stunted, tobacco-stained teeth. Several are missing or broken. His face is so small I could cup it easily in my palms; his hand is no bigger than a child's. Yet he is old, I think. Not so old as Pappos, but my father's age, perhaps. His skin is leathery, gathers in hard folds at his knuckles, his elbows, the back of his neck. His brown, wiry body reminds me of the gypsies we saw crouched in the open flaps of their skin tents in the hills of Macedonia, eyeing the van sharply as we hurried past.

But Xaralambos is no gypsy. He lives in the village, where every morning and evening he fishes with the other men. In the afternoons, he tends his vines, which grow in a plot just beyond our van.

The first time he walked by, I looked up from my book and smiled, and he did too. As the days passed, our smiles dissolved to greetings, and we began to speak, neither one of us understanding what the other said. I brought out the dictionary my husband's father gave us when we set out on this long journey. Flipping through the onion-skin pages, I marked places with my fingers, strung together a crude sort of sentence from the words I found.

—You . . . to live . . . village?

The fisherman looked bewildered. I showed him what was printed in the book.

—Village, I said. —Village!

I jabbed at the miniature hieroglyphs on the page, saying the syllables over and over, stupidly, as if to beat the word into intelligible shape. My husband watched us warily. He preferred that we kept to ourselves, for he worried that once we understood what they said, they would ask us to leave their beach.

When the fisherman finally spoke, what he said sounded nothing like what was printed in the book. He gestured to himself, to me, made motions with his hands. Finally, he took the dictionary from me, handed it to my husband, and broke a stick from the bamboo hedge. He drew pictures in the sand, printing words underneath. I repeated after him, marking my own words in the sand: *vivlio*, book; *dhentro*, tree; *xorin*, village. He put his finger on his chest. Xaralambos, *antras*, man.

Since then, every afternoon when he finishes his work in the vineyard, Xaralambos stops to speak. In the beginning, my husband sat with us, as if to chaperone, but now he naps with our son in the back of the van while I wait for Xaralambos in the shade, ordering in my mind the words I want to learn.

I point to the drawing, then to the horizon. – *Xrismos*, I say. – Hills.

– Hills.

He gets it right on the first try.

We have no rules for this game. I wish I had named the hills "mountain" or "horizon" or "promontory." What word, I wonder, has he chosen to teach me? My dictionary lists thirteen Greek words for water, depending on where it lies, how it moves, what it touches. There must be as many, at least, for elevations of land. Where I inhabit the surface of words, Xaralambos mines a language as layered as soil, or the sea, lifting words from submarine caves where the voice of Apollo still echoes. Recognizing this, we limit ourselves to concrete nouns and verbs that describe the things we do. I walk. You eat. We swim. Beauty, love, pain, sorrow: these are still too much for me.

I have exhausted my word list for today. I peer out of our shade, looking for another object to name. All I see is a yellow rubber dinghy approaching in slow bobs and jerks along the slender finger of land that points to the oracle on the other side of the sea. I reach for the packet of cigarettes lying in the sand. I offer one to Xaralambos, the only payment he allows, and take one for myself. I bend toward the match that he strikes and inhale deeply, as if every breath were another word. Relaxing in the shade, we repeat what we learned this afternoon. Our words, alternating Greek and English, mimic the give and take of conversation. *Yinaika*, woman; *paralia*, beach; *thalassa*, sea; *xrismos*, mountain, or horizon. Oracle, perhaps. I can't be sure.

As we speak, the dinghy bobs closer, a tic in the corner of my eye. Two shapes are visible, black against the late-afternoon sun, one rowing, the other small like a child. They cannot possibly hear us, but we lower our voices just the same. By the time they reach shore, we are whispering.

The woman who steps out of the dinghy is wearing a bikini of some reflective fabric that shifts like mercury in the sun. She is petite, as brown as Xaralambos, though her skin is soft and shiny with oil. Her stomach is flat, the navel collapsed to a thin crease. I am alarmed by her body, it is so hairless, so lacking in breasts and hips. I have been too long in the south, I think, where women are round, luxuriant.

Xaralambos is already padding down the beach, the cuffs of his trousers banging at his bare ankles. I stub out my cigarette and move into the sunlight. The man and the woman are German, I think. I decide this before they speak, though I can't say exactly why. Something about the set of their mouths. Or perhaps it is the man's belly, ponderous over the scrap of scarlet swimsuit that droops between his legs.

We dip into a common pool of language, settling, to my disappointment, on English. They are from Bern, Switzerland, holidaying at a resort on the other side of the point. They have been coming to this beach for twenty years, they say. We stand awkwardly in the overripe sun, our backs to the sea, digging holes in the sand with our toes. The coarse hair on the man's chest glistens with sweat. I answer their questions briefly, just short of being rude. I want them to leave.

   –Canada, I say.

   –Just travelling.

   –A year, more or less.

As I reply, I glance anxiously back at the van, every minute expecting my husband to appear and invite these tourists into our shade. But by the time I see him stirring, they are already pushing their dinghy back into the waves.

Our days on the beach near Rhodini have lengthened to weeks. We had misunderstood our compulsion to escape Athens. It was the city with its crush of tourists we despised. We have no desire to leave Greece.

   In the afternoons, others from the village join Xaralambos and me on the sand. Vassili, a university student close to my own age, home from Athens for the summer, and Demosthenes, who sits on the fringe of our shade. When we are introduced, I repeat his name and he corrects me, insisting that I lay the accent where it belongs, on the next-to-last syllable.

   The black eyes that glint like jet in Vassili lie smouldering in Demos's bare-boned face. He is too tall for a Greek, tightly strung. I often see him wandering the beach, almost always alone, mumbling to himself like the philosopher whose name he bears. His cousin Vassili treats him with reluctant tolerance, as if he's an annoying younger brother. Yet Demos seems old, much older than the rest of us, old as the limestone hills that rise from the beach. Vassili is handsome, but it is

Demos I am drawn to, just as I am drawn to the grandfather, Pappos; to my fisherman-teacher, Xaralambos; to the invisible temple of Delphi; and to this language with its layers of meaning that I am learning to speak.

My husband, restrained as always with strangers, sits on the running board of the van and sketches while my Greek friends and I repeat words softly to each other, hushing our laughter so as not to waken the little boy who sleeps inside. My son loves this place, the perpetual beach, the warm, shallow water with fishes that nibble his toes, and the people, always smiling, who make a fuss over his white-blond hair, his blue eyes, giving him sweet things to eat, cuddling him lap to lap. I love it here too, though I temper my enthusiasm for fear my husband will disapprove, or worse, misunderstand my affection for the place as an attraction to some particular person. I keep an eye on his mood, withdrawing my attention from the others when I sense he feels excluded.

Sometimes Vassili brings his younger sister, Andrea, to our beach. She is beautiful, with rounded breasts and hips and a belly that rolls and swells like the sea. She tires quickly of our language lessons and dives into the water, swimming to a rocky shoal just offshore. There, she slips a small knife from the waistband of her bathing suit and pries mollusks off the rocks, loosening the sea-flesh from the shells with her thumb, flicking the bits into her mouth, swallowing them whole.

Once, when we are swimming together, away from the men who watch us from the beach, she loosens a black mollusk and holds it out to me. I want to eat what she offers, but I hesitate before the slimy grey flesh. I think of Demeter, the goddess who ate Pelops, the Greek who gave this peninsula its name. Pelops was roasted and served to the gods by his father, Tantalus, who hoped to ingratiate himself with such a sacrifice. But Demeter recognized the taste of human flesh and warned the others, who restored Pelops to life. Tantalus they hung upside down from a tree, where he dangled forever over water he could not drink, reaching for fruit that always drifted from his grasp.

The mussel looks too much like raw flesh to me. I move my head up and down. – *Ohi*, I say. No.

After two weeks of instruction, I still have to pause to co-ordinate this simple response. The Greeks nod their heads agreeably when they say no, shake them side to side when they say *nai*, which means yes. This seems more foreign than the words themselves: the wistful, resigned yes, *nai*; the affirmative *ohi*, no.

We spend the whole afternoon away from the men, gathering mollusks, Andrea pausing now and then to slide one between her lips, smiling as she swallows as if to show me what I'm missing. When she picks up her things to leave, I offer her our harvest, but she refuses. Lacking the language of compulsion, I keep the pail of mussels. We eat them that night, carefully scrubbed and dredged in flour, fried golden in the olive oil Pappos brought, but they are tasteless and tough.

Demosthenes has been gone for days. He said he would be back *avrio*, which I understood as tomorrow, but time to the

Greeks is vagabond. They live in the present. *Avrio* is the future, any future, indeterminate, imprecise. He returns one morning, walking down the empty beach, hunched and distracted as usual, wearing black pants, a blue short-sleeved shirt, and leather shoes, the clothes obviously new but slightly rumpled, as if he'd slept in them overnight. He invites me to sit on the rocks near the water's edge, where we watch my son dig holes in the sand.

Demos has brought me a gift, an English-language newspaper. It is the first one I've seen in months, and it feels foreign in my hands. So many words blacken the page. I have come to savour arrangements of letters in isolation, scratched into sand or rolled bit by bit on the tongue before they are released into the air.

I cannot bear to read it. I look at the pictures instead. There is one on the front page that I recognize. I have seen this man many times before, rows of black-and-white images of his face pasted like filmstrips on hoardings in Athens, *Ohi Ohi Ohi* scrawled across each one.

"Papadopoulos," the caption says. Demosthenes jabs with his finger at the story underneath. Reluctantly, I read. The junta has consulted the people, and the results of the referendum are clear. The monarchy is officially abolished; the Republic of Greece has been declared. Democracy, promise the generals, is just months away.

Demosthenes spits into the sand. — *Psema!*

I don't understand.

— Lies. No democracy for Greece.

He pronounces "democracy" like his name, with the accent on the next-to-last syllable. His English surprises me. He holds up two fingers on his right hand. He wiggles one.

– Papadopoulos.

Then the other.

– America.

He entwines the two fingers tightly and waves them in my face.

– Papadopoulos and America. Like this.

My hands smooth the newspaper in my lap. The heat of the day is rising. It is time to retreat to my shade. Demosthenes is agitated. I want him to go away. But he keeps on talking, his voice shrill. The words are English, but they are so mangled by his strange inflections that I can't understand what he says. My son is watching us. His hole is filling up with water, which slowly collapses the sand.

Demosthenes puts his hand on my arm and speaks more slowly. – I am student at university. We make protest. Two years I am in prison.

He pauses, searching for words. – Amnesty. They release us. In *Avgustos*. For voting.

I remember seeing the posters on the hoardings, drinking carbonated lemonade from bottles as we watched soldiers, rifles at their chests, marching a line of men into a house on the far side of the deserted square. The black-robed women and old men who always sat under the trees by the fountain were gone. At church, we guessed, or on holiday. A truck inched down the empty street, its loudspeaker urgent. We listened, uncomprehending, and sipped our *limonadha*. We congratulated ourselves on eluding the tourist crowds.

I fold the newspaper in my lap and make a mental note for Xaralambos: newspaper, soldier, city square.

Demosthenes is not finished. He is pulling at the buttons of his shirt. I look away. Except for my son, we are alone on the beach. My husband has gone to the next village to sketch. Xaralambos is fishing with the village men. Andrea is inside with the women, embroidering pillow slips and tablecloths. I smile at my son to reassure him. But I can no longer avert my eyes from what Demos intends for me to see.

He is holding open his shirt, exposing his chest. Three scars slash through the tight mat of black hair between his nipples. He says the word distinctly. – Torture.

I look at the scars. I have never seen skin so silvery, so slick. What makes marks like these? A whip? Hot iron? Dull knives? I want to touch the raised, hairless flesh.

– My friends, they are in prison. Some die, he says, fumbling with the buttons of his shirt. – I am outside. I die too.

I have nothing to say. I have no words for this, not in his language or mine. I turn away from Demosthenes and look across the sea, longing for a glimpse of Delphi, the barest hint of what Apollo knew, but in the heat rising off the water, even the hills have disappeared.

We sit at a small square table in the whitewashed room on the hillside above the sea, myself and three men: my husband,

Vassili, and Demosthenes. Vassili brought us here, to his grandparents' house. – To see the real Greece, he said.

An old woman, his grandmother, I think, brings a tray with a bottle of ouzo and four small glasses. We were introduced when I entered the kitchen from the hard dirt yard where chickens scrabbled for insects between the donkeys' legs, but when Vassili said her name, the syllables slid by too quickly for me to grasp. As she sets a glass in front of me I try to catch her eye, but she does not look at me. I watch her disappear into the back room. Through the curtained doorway wafts the scent of frying oil and fresh bread. I want to follow her into the deeper reaches of the house, where Andrea has gone and taken our son, but I am a guest. I go where I am told.

Vassili pours the thick, clear liquor and we raise our glasses, clinking them together, *Eia!* We drink. The old woman offers us platters of fried cheese and goat's liver, ripe olives, long sticks of saltless bread that we tear off to mop up the sharp green oil. I chew deliberately, hoping to slow the flow of food from the kitchen. They will give us all they have, and I am afraid they do not have much. The hills we climbed to get here were barren except for bushes of scrub thyme and occasionally a twisted olive tree. The gods of these wild places, Pan and Dionysus, must have carved that second inscription on the temple at Delphi one winter while Apollo was away: Nothing Too Much. When I'd studied the myth, the teacher had said the phrase meant, "all things in moderation." But the hill people of Peloponnesus take the words to heart. Nothing is too much. The burden of their hospitality rests heavy with me.

The bottle is half empty. Vassili speaks of *Hellas*, the mountains and the sea. My husband sits with his chin in his hands, listening, memorizing, I suspect, not the young man's words but the curve of his nostril, the robust arch of his brow. Vassili might have stepped off a marble frieze, his features are that classically Greek. Demos sips at his glass of ouzo and stares at the sea far below. I follow his eyes to the water, a wash of blue tinged with gold by the raking afternoon light. Beyond, I can see the twin peaks of Mount Parnassos, sharp against the sky. Somewhere in the folds of its southern slope lies Delphi. Within the temple, the sacred rock, the sacrificial pit, the christening spring that opens the heart, fulfils the soul.

I turn back to the three men sitting in the shadowed room, Vassili declaiming, my husband listening, Demos distracted from both of them and silent, as he always seemed to be in company. I remember a poem from the book he had given me that morning, pressing it into my hands, saying, –Yannis Ritsos. In my prison too.

> The three of them sat before the window looking
>   at the sea.
> One talked about the sea. The second listened.
>   The third neither spoke nor listened; he was
>   deep in the sea; he floated.
>   . . . .
> The third one looked at them helpless from the
>   bottom of the sea, the way one looks at
>   drowned people.

Demos shifts his eyes from the window and stares at me. The words of the others are muffled by the roaring in my ears. I can't think how to speak to the dead.

When we leave, Andrea hands me my son, then pulls a thin bone ring from her finger and slips it onto mine.

— *Fila*, she says.

I know this word. — *Nai*, I say, shaking my head. — We are friends.

I have nothing to give her in return. It is not required, but still, I long to reciprocate in some way. I point to her, then to me.

— You come to Canada, visit me.

And she shakes her head, smiling. — *Nai. Nai.*

It is the Feast of the Assumption of the Holy Virgin. Xaralambos has invited us to a *glendi* in a neighbouring village. We all pile into the van, Xaralambos, his wife Zathanasea, Demos, Vassili, Andrea. Demos gives my son a gift, a string of worry beads, *koumbouloi*, and shows him how to slide his fingers over the red plastic spheres strung on the leather thong like a rosary.

When we arrive, the party is already underway. Long tables lined with men, women, and children criss-cross the square. Waves of laughter and song wash into the streets. We squeeze through the crowd, pausing often for greetings, introductions. Some friends of Xaralambos move closer together, making space at the table for us all. Bottles of *retsina* are opened and emptied into glasses. Andrea brings me a plate heaped with *dolmathes*, *salata*, and slabs of meat, fragrant with lemon and rosemary, sliced off the lamb that turns slowly on a spit at one side of the square. We gnaw at the bones, sucking the marrow noisily from the hollows, throw them into the straw at our feet.

On a makeshift stage, a band is tuning up: clarinet, drum, and stringed instruments I do not recognize. — *Bouzouki, santouri*, Xaralambos explains.

The music whines, its uneven rhythms undulate. In a small, cleared space in front of the musicians, women dance, holding their hands above their heads, snapping their fingers, old faces flushed above sombre clothes, young women swaying, their cleavages damp, eyes half closed as their feet lift in ancient steps. Andrea takes me by the hand and we join the circle of women, dancing round and round until the stars seem to spin. Then the men at our table get up to dance, all but Demos and my husband, who sit apart from us and watch.

When Vassili and the men return to our table, he motions with a slight nod across the square. Two foreign faces move through the crowd: the Swiss couple from the beach. They wave and head toward us, smiling.

— *Kako pedhi*, hisses Vassili.

Xaralambos would have been content to name only objects and colours, our movements on the sand, but Vassili was impatient. He'd taught me words of opinion and desire, of judgment. *Pisteio*: I believe. *Thelo*: I want. *Kalo* and *kako*: good and evil, the moral world of the Greeks cleaved by a single consonant.

— *Kako?* I ask.

Vassili says yes, and I wonder, Bad because they are tourists? But so am I. Because they speak German, then? In this country, the past is as fluid as the future. Hitler's fascists, the junta's coup, our visit to the hills: the events of half a century, all of them, yesterday.

— *Turistas?* I ask. — *Germanos?*

Vassili, always the spokesman, explains. — *Paralia . . . camera . . . pornographia.*

And I remember one day shortly after I met them, I saw their yellow dinghy moored at the far end of the beach, near where the Greeks threw their fishing lines into the sea. Xaralambos had been showing us how to dangle a hook from a square of cork, loop the line in circles in the sand, then whirl the cork over our heads, casting it far into the waves, trawling it back, snagging a snapper or perhaps a dogfish shark. The Swiss couple came out of the fig grove, onto the sand, their arms around each other, laughing, a movie camera slapping at the man's shoulder. Xaralambos had been reserved but not unfriendly, and he waved goodbye as they pushed off. We left a short time later, when a crowd of boys who'd followed the couple out of the grove surrounded the fishermen, talking excitedly, gesticulating toward the trees. We hadn't understood what was happening then. We do now.

The man and woman reach our table.

— Good evening, they say in English. — May we join you?

I bend to my son and wipe the lamb juice off his chin, hoping their words are not addressed to me. But no one else answers. Not my husband, not our Greek friends. I feel designated by their silence to reply.

—We are just about to leave, I say.

As if they've understood, the others gather their things, making good my lie. We leave the couple standing there. The *bouzouki* wails behind us as we find a *taverna* nearby where we can drink and dance. There is no roasted lamb and no straw under the table here, only plastic lanterns slung across a patio over young couples wriggling to more familiar, modern rhythms. My son lies asleep in Vassili's arms.

When Theodrakis begins to sing, Demos takes me to the dance floor.

— A great man, he says, his lips close to my ear. — His songs, they are the poems of Ritsos.

Demos is drunk and so am I. He draws me near. I feel him, hard, pressed against my thigh. Shocked, I pull away, just enough to define the borders of what's allowed. He's misunderstood my interest. It is not the intimacy of a man I seek, it's the soul of a people.

The days have grown cool. More than a month has passed since we arrived at Rhodini. In another week, Vassili and Demos will return to Athens, to university. My husband and I talk about where we'll travel next. We had intended to spend the winter on a kibbutz, but we like it here. We think perhaps we'll stay. Xaralambos needs help with the grape harvest, and it seems likely my husband can earn some money selling his drawings in nearby towns.

Within days of coming to this decision, however, we hear alarming news from tourists passing through Rhodini.

The Arabs have declared an embargo on oil, which has sent the price of gasoline skyrocketing. Airfares have doubled. Economists are warning of global collapse, and war with the Middle East seems certain. Suddenly, we are afraid of being trapped in this journey, forced to make this place our home. We have hardly thought of our parents, our sisters and brothers in Canada for months. They don't even know exactly where we are. We've been careful to keep our distance, jealous of the freedom we've found away from those who've known us all our lives. But these stories change everything. If Armageddon is upon us, we want to be near our own. We decide it is time to go.

We prepare the van for travel, take our last walks along the beach and up into the hills, say our goodbyes to the shopkeepers we visited every day, buying bread and meat and milk. On our last night on Peloponnesus, Andrea comes to our beach. For the first time, she is alone. We have built a small fire on the sand. She sits with us under the full moon that lights a path across the water.

Andrea hands me a paper on which she has written her name and address. She motions for me to do the same. She lays her hand across her heart, promises to visit me in Canada one day.

—No mussels there, I say.

— *Thempirazi*, she laughs.

It doesn't matter.

Just then, Vassili strides out of the darkness and I wave, smiling across the sand. But he does not look at me. He grabs Andrea by her elbow, jerks her to her feet, and speaks to her sharply.

— What's wrong? I ask, getting to my feet, too.

Andrea, agitated, traces brisk circles over her head then crosses her wrists over her breasts. She runs off, crying. My husband and I awkwardly brush the damp sand from our clothes. Vassili shakes our hands and says a formal farewell.

I am afraid my husband was right. We have overstayed our welcome.

Later, Xaralambos, Pappos, and Demos come to say goodbye. We stoke the fire with stalks of bamboo and olive-wood and pass wine that Pappos has made. Xaralambos wanders away and comes back with a handful of leaves, which he throws onto the flames. The air turns sharply fragrant.

I ask him what Andrea meant by her pantomime, and I repeat her gestures, drawing circles over my head and crossing my wrists. He points to his wedding ring, then ticks off on his fingers, — *Septemvrios, Octovrios, Noemvrios.*

I can't make any sense of it. I grow impatient with the charade and retrieve the dictionary from the van. Xaralambos flips through the pages and hands the book back to me, his finger pointing to a word with only one meaning: betrothed. He points to his watch, to my husband and me. Finally, I understand. A young woman promised in marriage cannot be alone on the beach at night. Not with strangers. Not with my husband, not with me.

All those afternoons, sifting through layers of language with Xaralambos, Vassili, Demos, and Andrea, I had come to think of them as friends, but now I have hit something hard, impenetrable. I can go this far, no further. These are not my people; this is not my place. After everything is said and done, I am still a stranger here.

I move closer to my husband, lift my son onto my lap. I want to say I am sorry, for her and for me, but I find only the word for sorrow. It will have to do. — *Lipi*, I say. — *Lipes*.

Xaralambos shrugs. Pappos has picked up my husband's guitar and is strumming two notes, an insistent minor chord around which he weaves a song without words. Xaralambos unties the scarf from his neck and reaches out to Demos. When he hesitates, Xaralambos pulls him to his feet. They each take a corner of the salt-stained cloth and, as we sit in the darkness and watch, they lift their feet on the pebbled sand to the thin wail of music that drifts across the sea, across to Delphi.

The next day, we drive to Patras and board the ferry to Bari, then drive straight north through Italy into Switzerland, stopping to sleep in parking areas and highway pull-offs, eating the last of the packaged soups and tinned sardines, buying only bread and milk and gasoline. The beach at Rhodini quickly fades. When we pool all our stray *drachmae*, *kronor*, *lire*, *Deutschmarks*, and *francs*, we calculate that if the price of fuel does not escalate too sharply, we can just make it to the village in southern Bavaria where my husband's grandparents live. From there we will wire for money to buy our tickets home.

When we awaken on the edge of a farmer's field somewhere in the Alps, frost whitens the windows of the van. The
sky is barely light, but we are so intent on getting home that
sleep seems a distraction. We leave our son on the mattress
and silently move to our seats in the front.

—If we start right away, I whisper, we can make Germany
by noon.

We drive into a long, narrow valley, perfectly flat. It is as
if, having created such grand precipices, God dragged his
finger between the peaks to make a small, smooth space to
rest the eye. As I look out my window, the side of a towering
mountain opens. What I took for a shadow on the slope is a
wide, dark door that now lifts like a portcullis. A jet painted
in camouflage is slowly nosing out.

— Stop! I shout, but my husband is already braking,
pulling the van sharply off the road.

We stare, dumbfounded, as the airplane rolls out of the
mountain, onto the highway in front of us, and takes off.

The door in the mountain has closed. The slope is once
again in shadow. The jet stream slashing white across the blue
morning sky could be a cloud. Already I doubt what I'm
certain I have seen.

— Let's stop for milk at the next village, I say quietly.
—Surely someone there will be able to explain.

But when we pull into the cluster of low, wooden chalets,
we see men in military drab jog-trotting down the cobblestones, rifles held stiff to their chests, not a civilian in sight. I
haven't read a newspaper since that day on the beach when
Demosthenes showed me his scars. Anything could have

happened. Some disaster. An emergency. War. My husband says nothing, but I know this is what he's thinking. As always, imagining the worst.

— There's a bakery, I say. — I'll get us some breakfast, find out what's going on.

The baker is square-faced, with a belly that hangs low over his belt. He looks exactly like the man who rowed the yellow dinghy to the beach at Rhodini, and for a minute, I think it's the same man, but that couldn't possibly be true. The phantom jet has unhinged me.

I point to the soldiers marching past the shop window and raise my eyebrows in question. Although I understand a smattering of French and German, I can make nothing of his reply. It must be his accent. I am completely disoriented: he sounds like he's speaking Greek.

I hear a rumble on the cobblestones outside. Tanks. My heart leaps to Demosthenes, to the students barricaded inside the Athens Polytechnical School, broadcasting their appeal: Rise against your oppressors. The junta's army has gathered on the hotel roof across from the school, the tanks are breaking open the iron gates, crushing them against the cobblestones, drowning out the students' screams: Stop, we are your brothers.

The baker smiles broadly, continuing to speak in his odd language. Something in the cadence of what he says tells me this is just an exercise. A military manoeuvre. A mock battle. A war game. The fear that grips me is not a premonition. This is not the real thing at all.

TAKEN FOR DELIRIUM

—∿—

My affection for the north country catches me unawares. Some disregarded part of me stirs unmistakably the moment I lay eyes on the spindly balsam firs, the grey, foreboding rock. I resist the attraction, for the features of this place are obviously homely, unappealing to someone like myself who loves the tropics, landscapes that gush and flaunt. I think perhaps the cold beauty of snow cupped in green boughs charmed me that day in the dead of winter when we bought the wooded acreage, but as spring melts the snow and shoulders of granite shrug out of the ground, my desire only deepens.

—You come by it honestly, my mother says, when I speak of the connection I feel to this chilled and barren land.

A century before, my great-great-grandmother, Margaret Cornfoot, left her cottage in Pittenweem, Scotland, sailed to

Canada, and walked north with her grown children from the end of the rail line into the wildwood to a scrap of land they'd bought, sight unseen, not too far from where I, myself, have come. The trees then had crowns so broad they blocked the sky, and trunks that four men, hand to hand, could not embrace, and the rocks still lay in wait under a scrim of soil.

It was never anything but a stone farm, and yet they stayed. After the highlands and the sea of her homeland, what had Margaret found to love in this spare forest and recalcitrant rock, this landscape so exacting and restrained? Was she, like me, drawn by its indifference?

I need to know this place, I can't say why.

Every day, after my older son climbs onto the school bus and my husband drives into the city to teach art at the college there, I put my baby boy on my back and walk into the bush. I spend the morning hauling skeletons of old cars, piece by piece, from the logging trails behind the house, telling myself that I, too, am clearing the land. One day a steering wheel, a trunk lid the next, then a fender, a rotting chassis, a hood that I drag by its corroded ornament to the road. Once, I find a windshield that I position in my garden in front of the bunching onions to give them an early start.

It is not just the decomposing wrecks that beckon me day after day into the woods. Inside the rotted hulk of a wartime Dodge, coils of green poke up through the back seat. A twining plant with spiny gourds embroiders a bumper. Underfoot, clusters of dark, glossy foliage soften my step: the red berries, when I press them between my fingertips, smell faintly of mint. There are loftier plants too, with slender May-green fronds that wave over shorter berry stalks. I want to know them all, to call them by name.

At a used-book store in the city, I find pocket books that describe flowers and shrubs and trees, with photographs and drawings of barks, berries, and leaves, systems for distinguishing one from another. Soon my parka pockets bulge with field guides. As I walk, I speak aloud the names of my new neighbours, the fiddleheads and wintergreens, the larches, hawthorns, and sarsaparilla. Birdsong remains a chorus of indistinguishable whistles and calls, but soon I recognize by sight the jays and owls and four kinds of grosbeaks that live in our woods, and even the warblers that travel here to raise their young.

The dog comes with my son and me, and sometimes the cat, following along the path at a discreet distance. In summer, my six-year-old son comes too, though less frequently as he finds paths of his own in the woods. My husband rarely joins us; he prefers to clear underbrush from the maple syrup grove or mow the rough grass in the clearing around the house, defining ever more precisely the place where we live. I don't mind. Every day, the landscape is becoming more mine; every day, more distinctly itself.

I find no more rusted metal to justify my daily ramble, but still I continue. These walks become my secret passion. I look forward to each one as I would to an illicit rendezvous.

I rush through my chores, struggling to clear a space in the late afternoon, a time when the light moves me as once I was moved by the light of early morning, a time no longer my own. I dig up the garden beside the house and plant vegetables, start a potato patch at the back, big enough to see the family through the winter. I harvest and stew the rhubarb and weed the quack grass that chokes an old asparagus bed, set up a corner of the shed for mail-order chicks: a flock of layers and another two dozen birds to kill in the fall for meat. I learn how to make soap from the drippings I save, and to churn butter from the cream I skim off the pail of milk I lug from the farm down the road.

I consult *Mother's Remedies*, a turn-of-the-century home-makers' manual I'd found among my favourite great-aunt's things when she died, and, according to its instructions, I plant camomile to soothe my young son's colicky stomach, a hedge of wormwood to keep mice from the cellar, marigolds to hang in bunches by the door against mosquitoes, and patches of mint, yarrow, and clary sage for tea.

We have little money, but we make a virtue of it, getting by with a resourcefulness handed down to me from my mother and, I like to think, from Margaret Cornfoot too. My days are clogged with work. I grow most of what we eat, the rest I buy in bulk: hundred-pound bags of flour and of sugar, bushels of peaches that I put up in Mason jars, and barrels of apples that I wrap and store in the dug-out cellar underneath the ramshackle little house. My husband cuts trees in the forest. Our older son and I stack what he splits, building a wall of firewood that stretches from the kitchen to the shed.

The formula we devise is simple. I look after the children, the chickens, and the gardens, he works a few days each week to earn money to pay for the land, and the rest of the time he devotes to his art.

The arrangement suits me well. I stand in the cellar as the first snow falls and admire the shining rows of pickles and tomato juice, jellies, chutneys, and chili sauce made from my mother's recipe, carrots buried in boxes of sand, braids of onions and garlic suspended from the joists, mounds of squash and gunny sacks of potatoes raised off the earthen floor on wooden pallets, and on the bottom step, a crock of sauerkraut, its sharp fragrance mingling with the scent of the cool, damp soil.

In winter, the workload lightens and I wander the woods with a clear conscience, my baby asleep on my back. I delight in the simple silence, only slowly coming to know the faint signs of inconspicuous life. A patch of bark rubbed bare by antlers. Higher in the conifers, pale evidence of porcupines. Crushed boughs where white-tailed deer passed the night. The hieroglyph of print and spoor in snow.

As the days lengthen and warm, my time is once again curtailed. There are maple trees to tap, and brush to collect to feed the fire that boils syrup all day long, tomato and pepper seedlings to start for the garden. I have to sneak away from chores that never end, stealing half an hour, sometimes more, at the end of the day, before the school bus pulls up to the mailbox, before a thin rise of dust marks the turning of my husband's car onto our concession road.

Early in the second spring, as I rush to gather eggs before the afternoon light fades, reluctant to do without my walk again, I lose my footing. My legs slip out from under me, and I fall, landing hard on the log that forms the henhouse stoop, my spine cracking against its squared edge.

When the first black wave of pain subsides, I see my little boy toddling toward me, rubbing his blanket against his cheek. I try to speak, to reassure him that I am all right, but I cannot.

There is no one for miles, no one expected for an hour at least. I begin to shake with cold. The light is dimming fast. My legs feel numb. I try to sit; fresh waves of pain force me back. Steeling myself, I roll onto my side. By using my arms in a sort of swimmer's crawl, I pull myself toward the house, gasping as spasms like electrical shocks shoot up my spine and down my legs. My son is becoming frightened, and so I make a game of it. He lies down beside me and together we worm our way across the grass.

It takes almost an hour to cover the thirty feet from the henhouse to the kitchen. Hand over hand, I haul myself up the door frame, stagger from chair to table to doorknob to bed, where I collapse and where I remain for days that stretch to weeks. I lie there, useless, as the tomato seedlings wilt and die, as the time passes when the manure should be dug into the garden and the peas and lettuce planted, when the hardy fruit trees from the horticultural station should be heeled into the ground, when the Jerusalem artichokes should be harvested, the rhubarb thinned, the asparagus pulled. I cannot do my part, and so it remains undone.

While my husband manages the house and makes his art,

the boys keep me company on the bed. We make a holiday of my confinement. My young son draws me stories and the older one prepares tea and toast for me, plays simple, happy melodies he composes himself on the piano in the living room. More than anything, I miss the bush, for there is only one window in the room, a long, narrow pane, and from my bed all I can see is neatly mown grass.

Every day I test my strength, negotiating a slow turn from my back to my side, until finally, one day, I roll off the edge of the bed onto my knees on the floor. I crawl to the window, grip the sill with both hands, and, keeping my back hunched and my stomach muscles tight, raise myself up by the strength of my arms. Breathing deeply, I let my weight settle on my legs. At last, I stand. My sons cheer and I laugh as I weep with the pain, for I can see trees at the edge of the clearing, the green balms of Gilead, and the sight calms me a little for I think, now, that balance will return, that I'll go back to the woods again.

It is weeks before I walk with confidence. My husband worries about the uneven ground of the forest paths, warns me to stay at home, but while I was lying in bed recuperating, reading *Mother's Remedies*, I found a new reason for my excursions to the woods. The plants that grow wild there are more than lovely, they are useful too. The inner bark of the elderberry, steeped with cream, can cool a burn; the bruised leaves of plantain cleanse poison from a wound; a poultice of stone root relieves muscle strain.

Such practicalities give purpose to my obsession. I label paper bags with the names of herbs and roots I seek out, prepare drying racks and screens, purchase dark-coloured glass jars to store the powders, tinctures, and decoctions I resolve to make. But although I convince myself for a time that my daily pilgrimage is deliberate, the force of my compulsion soon overwhelms my plan. The paper bags lie forgotten by the kitchen door. Leaves and roots and berries crumble to dust in my pockets. I wander over our fifty acres, commiserating with the bladder campion on its name, giving the ironwood a friendly tap each time I pass, pausing to relieve the hazelnut and pin-cherry trees of their caterpillar shrouds.

Early in June, I lean a board across the little stream that flows at the edge of the evergreens near the house. I cross the makeshift bridge and ease myself through the dense growth of alder, fir, and hemlock toward a clearing I thought I'd spied from the road, and I find it. An uplift of granite, perfectly flat on top, has made a spacious chamber in the woods, its rock floor so mottled with moss and lichens that when I squint my eyes the stone striates to marble.

Against this backdrop of sombre grey, a solitary pink flower catches my eye. It fairly glows. The plant itself is hardly noticeable: a slender, leafless stalk rising from an indentation in the stone so shallow it might have been made by the heel of my hand. But on top of the stem, two swollen, fleshy petals curve into each other, shaping a blossom that hangs taut and round as a small, luscious plum. For weeks, I've seen nothing but the chartreuse bells of Solomon's seal and pale umbels of wild leek. Now, suddenly, this blowsy bloom.

In a rush, the orchids of my childhood come back to me, clusters of pink and yellow flowers that stared out from behind lianas dangling in the *bosques* of Brazil. Their roots embraced the trees tightly. The crimson tongues thrusting from their painted petal faces seemed to speak to me, but though I made up stories, I never understood what they really said. Could this secluded flower rising from the granite be a distant relative of those tropical blooms?

I pull the field guide from my pocket and open it to the paintings of wildflowers in shades of pink. There it is, on the first page. Lady's slipper, *Cypripedium acaule*. It is an orchid, after all, a species from the tropics that flourishes in the north.

Later, back in my kitchen, I scour the bookshelf for *The Private Lives of Orchids*, a thin volume I bought at a yard sale for pennies, long ago on a whim. This particular orchid, I discover, grows in temperate places throughout the world. Yet everywhere its name is the same, derived from the shape of the flower that, for reasons I cannot fathom, others associate with shoes. *Frauenschuh. Sabot de la Vierge.* Early settlers to this country, no doubt Margaret Cornfoot too, called it moccasin-flower and squirrel's shoe.

I am disappointed. I turn to *Mother's Remedies* in search of something that might account for the effect this flower has on me, thriving alone in a stone clearing in the dense woods. And the orchid is there, called moccasin-flower, yes, and lady's slipper too, but also Noah's Ark, and at last a name that satisfies me: nerve root.

Gather. – In autumn, cleanse from dirt; dry in shade.
Part used. – The root.
Prepared (how). – In infusion.

Taken for delirium, the book says.

I come to measure the seasons by the plants and birds I
know. The tree sparrows fluffing their stick-pin breasts herald
spring. As the days grow warm, the wild calla unfolds its
white spathe by the stream. At midsummer, St. John's wort
blooms in the meadow, bouncing Bet sways in the ditches,
and chokecherries drip by the side of the road. Then the
Indian hemp opens its waxy pink bells and the pokeberries
whiten, and before long the vireos are gorging themselves on
bunchberries, and it is time once again to pick the pearly
everlastings before winter sets in.

I visit the orchid through all the seasons. After the flower
fades, shrivelling to a brownish-pink rag, the fruit swells,
poking its seed casing into the wind until the ribs split and
seeds like black sawdust sift into the autumn breeze. The
empty pod hangs on through the snow and in the spring, it
marks the spot where the plant will sprout again.

I can reach the stone clearing from the road but I prefer
to cross the grass beside the house, sidle over my makeshift
bridge, and ease through the evergreens along a path I made
myself, into the quiet chamber. As the weather warms, I fuss
over the patch of moss where the flower should appear,

barely able to restrain myself from digging in the soil to check for signs of life. Other mossy hollows play tricks on me, sprouting painted trillium and mayflower.

– It's been a year, I say to myself whenever the flower is late. – A lot can happen in a year.

But the orchid never fails me. One day in late May or early June, a pale green spike pushes up through the moss, its tightly wrapped leaves unfurl, and, at last, the flower that I've been waiting for blooms.

Year after year, as hard as I look, I do not find another orchid on our land. This does not surprise me, really. It isn't like other plants. It can only grow in symbiosis with a certain soil fungus, a relationship that must be well established before the orchid flowers. This particular species takes longer than any other, up to seventeen years.

The orchid in the clearing never sets more than a single bud. Once, shortly after it opened, I saw a bee disappear through a cleft where the petals folded into each other. I squatted on my hands and knees, scraping my shins against the granite, to peer closely at the shadow of the bee as it buzzed about inside. It seemed frantic at first, then grew quiet. I worried that it was trapped, but I waited, my knees stiffening, and finally it wandered out through an opening near the top. I recalled then something I'd once read, that prisons have pink rooms where the violent and deranged are calmed.

The sight of the lady's slipper restores me too. I go to see it often once the boys are both in school and my days are more my own. The hours are no longer consumed with caring for the house, with growing and preserving our food. I have become proficient at all these things, and so they take up less time, but they give me less satisfaction too. I hardly see my husband now, except at meals. Over the years he's become more and more absorbed in his work. After dinner, he heads straight to his studio, where he sculpts late into the night. We've grown steadily more distant. When arguments erupt, he says often now what he has told me in moments of anger throughout our married life, that a man can't be committed to both his family and his art. We always make it up, but after he leaves for his job and the children get on the bus, the empty house seems tainted somehow by our words. It is only in the woods, and especially there, crouched on the granite, that I remember what it is to feel content.

I visit in the days, and sometimes in the nights too, for I have taken up again an old habit from my childhood. I time my departure perfectly so that just as my husband reaches for me, I rise on a slender, silver thread, leaving my body on the bed as I fly high into the blackened sky, above the hemlocks and the balsam firs, drifting to the clearing, where I float above the stone and gaze down at the solitary flower, taking comfort from the staunch, secluded bloom.

One spring, when my older boy had just become a teenager, we are hauling a wagonload of rotted hay for the garden from a farm several miles away, my husband driving the tractor, the boys and me on top, when we see smoke, a sepia stain in the sky above the woods.

—Is it a forest fire? my older son asks.

—Will it burn down the house? adds the younger boy.

My husband tells them, — Don't worry, the wind is blowing the other way.

But I am not reassured. As we fork thick mulch between the rows of vegetables, I check the horizon. It darkens steadily to that eerie sulphurous hue that presages a thunderstorm or an eclipse. When the boys have had enough, I drive them to a friend's house, and on my way back I think I see the tips of flames leaping from distant trees. My husband says it must be a trick of the light. By noon, though, as we spread the last of the hay, we can both smell fire. I leave the garden to collect eggs for our lunch, and slip behind the chicken coop, into the woods. I have not yet lost sight of the house when the sting of smoke in my eyes forces me back.

My husband takes the tractor down a logging road to see how close the fire has come. I stay in the kitchen and pour myself a cup of tea. There is no fire department in this township. If the wind blows the flames our way, we'll burn.

I look around at the furniture, fix each piece in my memory, as if preparing myself never to see it again. The piano I bought for my older son, who shows such promise. The white-oak kitchen cupboard with glass handles and great rounded bins for flour and sugar, left to me by my great-aunt. The antique Scottish rocking chair, where I've rocked my babies and myself, too, from the time I was a teenager, when

I received the chair as a gift from an elderly couple whose house I used to clean.

Then my eye falls on the madonna and child that my husband carved, years ago, in Sweden. I can't part with that. Nor can I part with the watercolour I bought of a woman, her hair a wild tangle of curling flames, vines twining her breasts, the flesh on her arms shifting to fur, her hands transformed to paws that flex on wooden boards painted a deep, visceral pink.

Although we own many paintings, bartered for my husband's work, this is the only piece of art I've ever chosen for myself, paid for with the first money I earned from something I wrote. The moment I'd seen the painting in the gallery where my husband would soon exhibit, I knew I had to have it, for I recognized this lion-woman, the way one knows the face of a dimly remembered childhood friend or a figure that reappears in old family photographs. Someone not quite familiar but still close to the heart. The artist named the painting *Sphinx* and, it's true, this lion-woman seems wise, the answers to unnamed riddles concealed within her tranquil gaze.

I am setting the painting on the floor with a few other things, *Mother's Remedies*, the boys' baby books, my diaries, when my husband returns.

– The fire is on our land, he says, his voice calm, as if he has just said, The sun is in the sky.

I join him outside. The wind has changed. Now the air around the house is smudged grey with smoke. Above the trees I see the unmistakable flash of flame.

With our backs to the road, we don't see the cars until they pull up on the grass behind us, braking sharply, dozens of them, cars and pickups, tractors and wagons, one farmer with a manure-spreader full of water, everyone popping trunks and pulling out chainsaws, pickaxes, shovels.

– C'mon. We'll dig a fire line! one man yells at my husband, pushing with the others toward the bush, calling back to me, – Better get what you can out of the house. Pile it on the hay wagon. Someone'll drive it to a safe place.

The men shout at each other, spread out in groups of four or five to enter the woods. The urgency with which they move makes me think this danger must be real, yet I don't feel alarmed. I wander through the house, culling only what seems most precious, the brass candlesticks my parents gave us for a wedding present, our photograph albums, a few of our sons' favourite books and games. I pile them in the back seat of our car, together with the painting and the carving of the madonna and child. I feel a little foolish doing this, until the resinous scent of burning trees reminds me that something momentous is happening deep in the woods.

I telephone my mother and tell her we may lose everything. Saying the words finally shakes me from my lethargy. I take garbage bags into the bedrooms and stuff them with pillows and blankets stripped from the beds, all our clothes from the closets, hangers still attached. I haul bushel baskets up from the cellar and fill them with dishes layered in tea towels and bed linen. In less than an hour, our worldly goods, all but the heavy pieces of furniture, are packed and pushed onto the hay wagon. I visit the basement, for the last time perhaps. It is the only part of the ramshackle house where I feel the urge to say goodbye. The preserves in the pantry are too fragile to move. Besides, I've run out of boxes and baskets. I go outside and raise the hatch on the chicken coop, but the hens cower under the roost, reluctant to run free.

The smoke is thick among the trees now. I cross the little bridge and make my way to the clearing where the lady's slipper has just bloomed. I lie down beside it, my cheek against the granite. Here, the air still smells fresh. I listen to the buzz of chainsaws, the crash of trees in the woods. Even if the forest burns, I think, the stone with its fertile hollows will remain.

When I hear helicopters overhead, I make my way through the trees to the road. Men in orange overalls are hauling pumps to the stream, uncoiling hoses across the grass.

—Don't worry! one of them yells in my direction. —There's a truck coming to spray the house!

I start to shout my thanks but give up. He is intent on his work, strapping a portable sprayer on his back as he heads into the woods.

Out of the haze obscuring the trees, half a dozen men appear, hoisting something high on their shoulders. When they see me, they wave, —Look what we saved!

It is one of my husband's sculptures, an old woman cast in fibreglass, struggling forward in sorrow, her dead son's body draped across her arms, both of them larger than life, their limbs and faces distended, distorted in pain. It is the most ambitious of his renderings of mother and child, one he thought he'd abandoned forever, deep in the bush.

The fire that spring smouldered underground for days, but the forest survived. The flames had cleared the underbrush and licked clean the branches, yet before summer faded, the conifers were full again, wintergreen and lycopodium sprouted underfoot.

One fall, after the orchid sifts its seeds in the wind, I kill the chickens I'd raised for meat, and the laying hens too, for by now the flock is old and yellow-legged, not worth keeping alive through the coming months of bitter cold.

For hours I bend over the old maple stump, sliding one bird's neck after another between twin nails, severing the neck with a blow of the axe, tying up the birds by their feet to bleed, stoking the fire under the cast-iron kettle to keep the water at a rolling boil so the feathers will loosen at one dip. I slice smoothly down each breastbone and reach deep inside to finger loose the heart and lungs, sliding out the steaming guts with a single cup of the palm.

The killing and the cleaning take all day. As I pick up the last armload of bagged birds to take them to the freezer, something gives in my spine. I sink to my knees, a familiar shock of pain flashing down my legs. Once again I crawl to the house, but this time the weeks in bed extend to months. A doctor diagnoses a debilitating disease. – Stay mobile, he tells me sternly. – No matter how much it hurts.

And so I do. Every morning, I roll off the edge of the bed, pull myself to my feet, and shuffle up and down the hall until I no longer have feeling in my legs. In the afternoons, I haul myself to my feet again and make my slow way into the kitchen where, leaning on the counter, I prepare the evening meal. I learn to put the pain far away from me, consign it to a tiny red receptacle, where it stays as long as I have the will to concentrate. I rarely think of the orchid.

When I do leave the house, I am forced to use a wheelchair. One day, tired of being confined, I go to the shopping mall with the others. The boys, both of them fully adolescent now, take off on their own. I beg my husband to stay with me, but he leaves too, intent on whatever it is he has to do.

—But please . . ., I say, reaching for his hand.

—You'll be fine, he replies, avoiding my touch, walking away.

This is how our conversations go now, our words never quite finding a home, drifting off unrequited or, worse, trapped, ricocheting inside our own heads.

I sit in the plastic folds of the rented wheelchair and replay our argument of the night before, an echo of so many others. It erupted, as usual, after days of his hard-eyed silence, which had been triggered, I knew, by some neglect or oversight of mine, some unintended slight, perhaps, or some sign of interest in another man (or a woman), for despite all my years of utter faithfulness, he still maintains a jealous turn of mind. Finally, I took up my part, too. I urged him to explain, begging him with tears, until at last he made his accusations. Over the years, the litany of my shortcomings has changed, but it always ends the same. —I can't go on, he raged. —I can't be an artist and live with you.

My response, in all these sixteen years, has never varied. I convince him with my coaxing, and we are happy for a while, until my next misstep.

Sitting alone in the atrium of the mall, shoppers brushing past on every side, I find my lips shaping different words, a new reply, which I speak aloud to myself, as if moved by revelation. —I cannot be your wife and survive.

On the first day of June, my last day on the land, I walk with my husband to the clearing and show him the mossy hollow in the granite where the orchid will soon appear.

A year has passed since that day in the shopping mall. I am healthy again, but the familiar pattern of existence my husband and I once shared has been disturbed. During the summer and fall, the gardens kept me busy, and I returned to my walks in the woods. But then, as the days shortened, the weather grew cold, isolating me within his silence, and him within mine. When I met a man who said he wanted me, I did what I'd held unthinkable, and so gave credence to my husband's habit of suspicion. And in late winter, after a holiday with my girlfriend in Mexico, my first time away alone, my husband and I agreed at last to separate. All through the spring he searched for a place where he could live and make art, and when he failed to find something suitable, it was I who offered to leave.

Now my younger son and I are moving to a city several hundred kilometres to the south. My older boy, who is sixteen, has chosen to stay here, with his father. I tell myself I'm not leaving him behind: he'll always be with me, in the aching of my heart.

I do not know it yet, standing here with my husband in the clearing, but every year, near the end of May, something in me will stir. I will find myself yearning for granite, the rock that never flinches underfoot. I'll recall with longing the weedy balsams and their tenuous toehold in this indifferent place. And I will remember the orchid. I'll think, one day, that I liked her so well because she survived on so little.

My husband will build a garage on the uplift of granite; cars will drive into the clearing through the lane of balsam trees. Perhaps he will have forgotten the orchid that bloomed there every spring. Or perhaps he has already learned other ways to make the landscape his.

THE STILL POINT

—It could be an earthquake, says Sharon. —Maybe we should stand in a doorway or something.

Sharon, naked, is sitting on her haunches, her hands spread flat on the terracotta floor between her knees. At any moment, I expect her bum to rise in the air, her weight balanced on her elbows in one of those ridiculous positions that our gym teachers used to prod us into. The circle of red tiles in front of her fingers is slowly erupting. We were awakened a short while ago when the centre tile snapped in half; now it is canted three inches in the air.

I am lying on the bed, toes on the pillow, my head sticking out from a shroud of mosquito netting. The tiles are directly under my nose, where they continue to erupt, but gently, as if inflating with a deep intake of breath. The crack zigzags in slow motion in the direction of Sharon's round, blonde belly.

—Nothing else seems to be moving, I say, nodding toward the little glasses on the night table and the bottle on the dresser, all of which sit perfectly immobile, no tinkling, no telltale sloshing.

We, on the other hand, are more than a little sloshed. This is our first night in Zihuatanejo, and Mexican rum, we've discovered, is dark, tasty, and cheap. We may be sharing more than a spur-of-the-moment holiday: this could be a joint hallucination. Either way, I think, a little more rum won't hurt. I pour a couple of inches in each glass and hand one to Sharon.

—I guess we're not the only ones cracking up.

—To earthquakes, declares Sharon, raising her glass.

—To the earth moving, I reply.

That afternoon, as I walked across the tarmac from the airplane to the little terminal at Zihuatanejo, the low stucco building had wavered like a mirage. It wasn't just the heat. The asphalt that scalded the soles of my sandals, the smell of dust and baked diesel, the hills studded with palms, flushed golden in the slanting light: suddenly I was nine again, walking away from my family on the verandah of the *fazenda* in Brazil, heading for the tall grass and adventure, the air crackling with sunlight and possibility and now with something else as well: the ferment of memory.

I closed my eyes against the dislocating sun, stopped to run my fingers underneath my glasses, scraping away the sweat.

This was not Brazil, I reminded myself, it was Mexico. And I was no longer a child. But the excitement that bubbled inside me till I couldn't see straight, that was distinctly childish.

I felt giddy with sensation, unreasonably delighted, released from responsibility, ready for anything.

When I opened my eyes, the terminal no longer seemed to sway, and my best friend, Sharon, was hailing me from the other side of the customs barrier. The week of my escape had begun. For the first time in seventeen years of marriage, almost all my adult life, I was travelling on my own.

I have heard that climbing one mountain a hundred times can be as stimulating to the mind and heart as scaling a hundred different peaks. But surely it takes more out of you. Familiarity can be such an obstacle, assumptions overlaying one another until the true contour of the land is hopelessly lost.

I was tired of embarking on the same old arguments with my husband, worn out from reaching understandings that had to be reached again and again. So when Sharon suggested I join her for a week in Mexico, alone, I called the travel agent before I could marshal reasons why I shouldn't go.

A change of scenery would give me fresh perspective, I hoped, show me some new way to move ahead in the same direction. But I had forgotten what I'd learned early as a traveller, that shifting location alters everything. Even the usual laws of physics no longer seem to apply. How else to explain the tiny earthquake at the foot of our beds that resounded through the night?

– Do you think we should tell somebody? Sharon asks in the morning as we watch the sun rise, buoyant in a sangria sky.

I understand that this is not a question at all.

– If we put the luggage bench over it, maybe the maid won't notice when she makes up the beds, I suggest.

When we come back from our breakfast of crusty, fresh *bolillos* and cinnamon coffee, taken under a *palapa* at the ocean's edge, the mosquito netting is tied back neatly with hibiscus blossoms and a dotted line of red ants leads resolutely from the flowers, across the white bedspread toward a cockroach husk in one corner of the room. But the bench at the end of the bed has not been moved; our little earthquake is intact. We take this as a sign. We designate ourselves the keepers of the mystery, the sibyls of Zihuatanejo, and though we can't even keep a straight face as we bow to each other in mock reverence, I know I'm not altogether kidding.

– I'm going swimming, I tell Sharon. – Put in a good word for me with the powers that be.

It is not that I'm afraid of being drowned, but I admit the ocean makes me anxious. I have never got over a childhood mistrust of large bodies of water that move. The sound of the waves, which I know I should find soothing, disturbs me. The rhythm seems aggressive in its persistence, even on a quiet morning like this, when the tide is out and only the gentlest of curls roll in from the sea.

I thought that perhaps here, on the shore of the Pacific, I might overcome my apprehension, but when I get to the water, I decide just to walk along the edge, to let it wash over my bare feet. Now and then I pause, allowing the undertow to finger my ankles, scrabble at the sand under my toes until I sink a little, leaving two small footprints that the next wave

obliterates. There is something Sisyphean in the action of the
tide, carving a pattern in the sand, wiping it away, carving
another again. How do others find peace in this?

Slowly I skirt the bay, edging sideways into the water as I
walk, easing myself a little deeper, swaying with the waves as
they lap at my shins, my calves, my knees. I focus on the
water's movement, trying to detect the precise moment when
the tide hangs suspended, the rushing forward in perfect
balance with the pulling back. Time and again, I think I feel
it, a split-second respite, but it passes so swiftly I can't be sure.

I walk through the shallow water all the way to the end
of the beach and back, my head cocked as if listening for
voices, attuned only to the ebb and flow. I am oblivious to the
fishing boats that come in with their catch, to the tourists who
spread out on the sand as the sun mounts the sky. I don't give
up until Sharon calls to me from a *palapa* in front of the hotel,
and I reluctantly abandon my quest. But I promise myself
that before the week is out I will find that shifting interval,
the moment when the water holds perfectly still.

In the afternoon, as the heat of the day dissolves, we leave the
hotel and walk along the Playa de la Ropa toward the houses
that cluster in the bowl of the bay. Zihuatanejo was a fishing
village long before there were tourists to buy baskets and
beads. No doubt it has aspirations, but it is not yet Acapulco
or Cancún. There are no domino-rows of condos lined up
along the beach, no discos throbbing with gringos on week-
long passes from the cold.

Besides our hotel, there is just one other on this curve of sand, and only a handful of rooms on its ground floor are occupied. The walkways that circle the upper storeys are cordoned off, the concrete cracked and crumbled by the earthquake that rumbled through here three years ago on its way from Mexico City to the ocean.

At the far end of the beach stands another grand structure, its sprawling, pillared courtyards all but abandoned too. According to the maid who keeps our room well stocked with bottled water as an excuse to practise English, this was once the pleasure palace of Mexico's chief of police. Built for orgies, she says. We resolve to peek through its elaborate wrought-iron gates, but the villa is guarded by young soldiers who find their own carnal delight in contemplating the sunbathers splayed on the beach.

The walk into town takes us half an hour, past the deserted hotel and the pleasure palace, up a gully to the highway edged with flagrant bougainvillea. To reach the shops and the *zócalo* at the centre of the village, we have to cross the sewer, a raised concrete ditch that drains a sluggish inch or two of fetid liquid toward the bay.

—Look at this, Sharon calls ahead to me.

She has stopped on the bridge that spans the sewer and is waving a scrap of paper she's picked up from the ground.

— There's another one, I say, indicating the pavement between us. —And another.

The strips of paper look like they've been crudely torn from a school scribbler. They flutter along the sidewalk, blazing the way into Zihuatanejo. The Mexican women who pass us, their string bags stretched with tomatoes, onions, and red snapper, step over them without a glance. The children don't stop either, even though when I bend to pick one up I notice there is a coin taped to one side. On the other, someone has written several sentences; a young woman, I suspect, since the letters are round and full, almost adult, yet innocent.

–What does it say?

–I'm not sure, replies Sharon, stooping to collect another. –But they all seem to be the same.

I try to read the message. Spoken Spanish has such a familiar cadence that this morning I was lulled into believing I understood what the waiters were saying, but the written language keeps me humble. I can make no sense of this at all.

It is Sharon who translates. – It goes something like . . . The Virgin of St. John of the Lakes is the most powerful in all the world. If you pick this up and make a hundred copies and toss them around, within nine days the Virgin will bring you lots of money . . . and if you don't, you'll die.

– My god! she exclaims, dropping her fistful of notes. –It's a curse.

–More like a high-stakes chain letter, I say. –All I was ever promised from chain letters were recipes or postcards from strangers.

I fold the scrap of paper around the coin and slip it into the pocket of my shorts.

–You're not going to keep it.

– Are you kidding? Of course I am. And, no, I'm not going to spend the afternoon writing out a hundred copies and dropping them on the beach.

Sharon stares at me, horrified. Whether or not she believes, she never risks offending the gods. I, on the other hand, have learned to be so cautious around the people I love that it's a relief, with saints and angels, to let down my guard.

I put my arm around her waist. – Come on. Let's get some pineapple to go with that rum.

We are thirsty for the sun.

Every day from early morning until noon we lie comatose on the beach, our novels unread, unopened at our sides. The recycled-beer-glass bowl that we bought in the village is settled in the sand between us, filled with rum-drenched pineapple that we suck on like honeyed soothers.

Few words pass between us. There is too much to talk about. We are loath to bring to the beach the men and the children we've left behind, the heartaches, the quandaries we've set aside, and so we retire behind our dark glasses and rely on the sun to iron out our crumpled lives.

Hour after hour, I lie thinking of nothing at all, a condition so rare it seems almost like an illness, a lethargy induced by fever, until I open my eyes, see the glint of sun on the sand, and I sink back, blissful in my stupor. Occasionally I get up to stroll the water's edge, allow the waves to play with my toes, but this place has quickly worked its magic. It occurs to me that what obsessed me that first morning as I walked up and down the shore, resolved to isolate some fixed instant of tranquility, no longer matters. I can't even remember why I cared.

When the sand becomes unbearably hot, we retreat to our room and change into cotton shifts embroidered with Mayan deities. On the fourth day, made brazen by the heat, and anonymous in this landscape, we leave our underwear folded in our suitcases and walk up a path that leads into the hills, our skirts scooping cool breezes up our thighs.

It is winter, and the woods flicker with birds that headed south months ago. I watch a yellow warbler I know from the northern forest and marvel how at home it seems here, too.

– Have you noticed the shoes? says Sharon, interrupting my thoughts. She is standing by a sandal in the ditch. – That's the third one we've passed.

It seems that lately it's always Sharon who is scanning the earth, and me the sky. I've never thought of myself as ethereal. I am practical, and competent, the one whom others rely on to hold to the path. That is, until recently, when I've found myself more often looking to the heavens, to the constellations that shift through the vast, open sky. I've even taken to reading horoscopes and, what is worse, to scanning events for evidence of accuracy in their predictions. I recall now what was foretold for this week:

> The needs of your loved ones may seem more demanding than usual, but take nothing for granted; that which you are seeking will appear in a most unusual place.

– What shoes? I ask, mindful of the advice.

—They're all *left* shoes, she says, a little impatiently. —Don't you see? A running shoe, a flip-flop, a leather sandal? They're all left shoes. And look, there's another one.

She gestures ahead to a muddy pink Sunday shoe, a child's shoe, lying in the middle of the road. When we get to it, she kicks it over. —What did I tell you? Left foot again. It's weird, don't you think?

In the next mile or so, we count eight more left shoes. The amputee jokes are beginning to pall. Except for the birds and the shoes, we are alone on this path, which twists away from the beach up a barren slope scattered with dwarfish trees.

After a while we stop counting the shoes, though we both continue to glance furtively at the baked earth, puzzling over what the cast-off footwear might mean, if anything. A silence grows between us, oddly charged by this enigma. To break the tension, we begin to talk, not about this place but about the one we left, relieved to contemplate more familiar mysteries. She tells me her concerns about her daughter who is poised on the cusp of womanhood, and her worries about her lover's health, the sharp, uric smell of his skin. She pauses, and I know I must reciprocate, share secrets of my own. I do not break my habit of suppression easily, but once I begin to talk, it all comes rushing out: the bitter silences I've endured, the years of groundless accusations, the jealousies, suspicions. And feeling a shame more fitting to a woman of my mother's generation, I confess that I've been with another man, that I have turned my husband's unfair fictions into truth.

—Do you intend to leave him?

—No, I say, without hesitation.

She grins.

—Wait a minute. Which 'him' do you mean? I'm not ready to give up on my marriage, if that's what you're getting at. And I'd never leave my kids. I don't love this other man. But, how can I describe it? Being with him has changed me. I used to want to stay married no matter what, till death do us part and all that, but now I don't know for certain. I want to be married, but I want it to be better. It has always been such a struggle. I don't think my husband has *ever* been sure. Even after all these years, I have to keep convincing him that what we have can be good. Part of me just wants to let go, see what happens.

—Maybe you should tell your husband about the other man, Sharon suggests.

—Are you kidding? Never!

Our conversation stops abruptly. We've both noticed the boy at the same moment. He is standing beside a misshapen tree, hacking at a branch with a machete. Not hacking as if to cut it down, just a rhythmic *thwack . . . thwack . . . thwack*. He is only fifteen, maybe sixteen, the same age as my older son. What he is doing, I think, must be the rural Mexican equivalent of playing video games.

The path we are on winds close to the tree. It seems to end a few feet beyond, at a makeshift hut where a pig roots desultorily amidst debris. The boy doesn't look at what he is doing to the tree. He stares at us, and I sense by the boldness of his gaze that his eyes have been on us since long before we saw his face.

—Shouldn't we be getting back? I say, with careful nonchalance. —It must be almost happy hour.

As if on a signal, Sharon and I turn and start down the hill, the staccato beat of the machete sounding our retreat. At the bottom, instead of taking the path through the woods the way we came, we veer left, thankful for the cluster of late-afternoon bathers just barely visible at the water's edge. Stirred by longing for my sons, by curiosity, or by some sixth sense, I glance back up the hill, to the boy by the gnarled tree. Through the tangle of undergrowth, I see him, staring down at us still. The thwacking sound has stopped. The machete is limp in his right hand; with his left, he is pulling at himself, the rhythm sullen, unremitting.

I clutch at Sharon's arm. —Let's get out of here.

Every evening, the light, as it fades, clears the Playa de la Ropa, sweeping hotel guests toward the Japanese lanterns that circle the pavilion. The waiters and the tables wear starched whites. There are bouquets of red hibiscus and jugs of *piña colada* at every elbow. The buffet table that was at the centre of the pavilion, heavy with mango, melon, and kiwi earlier in the day, has been replaced by an electric organ, a one-man band of digital samba, polka, and salsa. The plump, grinning man at the keyboard has ambitions. After restrained renditions of "Tiny Bubbles" and "The Girl from Ipanema," he breaks into a thumping Latino version of "Twist and Shout," then, shrugging sheepishly in the direction of the hotel owner, he flips the switch to waltz and slides into "Que Sera, Sera."

The Chubby Checker hopeful angles to catch our eye, but

Sharon and I are having none of it. We choose our table care-fully: the small round one at the edge of the pavilion where we can look out at the shimmer of black ocean. A green parrot named José struts from chair to chair, cawing unintel-ligible phrases and caressing our legs with his beak, prancing and making a show of himself in exchange for bits of food.

– Isn't that just like a man? Sharon says, tearing off a corner of tortilla and holding it out to the bird.

At the *papelería* in town, we bought a sheaf of airmail tissue and now we sit in silence, distilling our days for those at home. I have already sent postcards to my sons, choosing a picture of a mariachi band for the older one, a musician, and a close-up of a pelican for the younger boy, who loves to draw.

I write first to the man I've been seeing, letting him know, in convoluted phrases of gratitude and resignation, that our trysts must end, for, whatever he means to me, it is nothing set against what I want for my sons. Then I write to my husband, in simple terms, of the clarity of the skies and the particular blue of the water, of how much I've appreci-ated this time away. I restrain myself from shaping my words to his demands so that I can take from him what I need, but I wonder, as I read over the letter, if he will understand that this, too, is an offering.

Sharon stands up to get the stamps from our room. As she passes, she puts her hand on my shoulder.

–So have you made a decision yet? she asks gently, letting her fingers stray across the top of my back and up my neck.

I lean into the palm of her hand. — About breaking it off with the other man? Yes. But I don't know if I have what it takes to keep the marriage going.

She bends over and reads the page on the table in front of me. She doesn't have to ask permission, she knows this is allowed.

— I see you've decided to tell your husband after all.

— What do you mean?

I glance down at what I have written. It is flawlessly cheerful. — I haven't said a thing.

— Oh yes, you have, she says, holding the letter up to the light.

Pressed into the paper, clearly legible under the blue ink of my message to my husband, are the embossed words of what I wrote to the other man. I snatch the page from her hand, grab a spoon, and rub tight circles over every inch of it, smoothing away my duplicity.

It is my last morning in Zihuatanejo. Sharon left yesterday, and now I am completely alone. The first light lures me out of my bed, over the pool of crumbled tiles, which, together with the abandoned shoes and the pleas to the Virgin, I hold as abiding mysteries, mementoes of all that's capricious, of what can't be known.

On the beach, near the water, the sand is cool and hard, dimpled with the air-holes of sea creatures abandoned by the tide. A warm breeze blows across my cheek, and I sniff at it, trying to catch the essence of the ocean, the hills, the trees. It smells of where I am, but also, like the tarmac at the airport, of where I've been.

The bay is deserted except for a cruise ship making its slow way toward the village where lights blink in the pale dawn. I follow the curve of the sand, moving away from the hotel, toward the police chief's villa, letting the waves wash over my feet one last time. I think again of the lull in the tide I was so anxious to find. Perhaps it exists only in theory, or in my mind, a calm that passes before it can be known.

All week I have avoided swimming in the ocean, but now I think I may not have another chance. I face the open water and walk into the waves, feeling them lap against my thighs, my waist, my breasts. A breaker, born far out at sea, rolls toward me, scooping up lesser waves like a liquid avalanche. I turn my back to it and wait, fighting the urge to look, to predict its force, its impact, to determine where it will carry me. Hoping that here, finally, I might learn the trick to letting go.

The water breaks over me and I allow myself to be swept along in its curl, my face buried in foam, rushing headlong to wherever the wave deposits me, gasping, while it rushes back, tickling my legs, tugging at me to follow. I kneel in the undertow, coughing and laughing, trying to get my breath, exhilarated, the sting of salt awakening my skin.

I slick my hair back from my eyes with one hand and, with the other, grab at the folds of my bathing suit, which the waves had tugged down to my hips.

A man's voice cuts through the sound of the ocean.

— *Buenos días*, he says.

Stunned by salt water, all I can see is a white grin in a dark face and the glint of a metal shaft. It is a soldier, sitting on a piece of driftwood, his khaki shirt open too far, hands cradling the muzzle of his rifle, the butt end resting in the sand between his legs.

I pull the straps of my bathing suit up over my shoulders with a shrug and turn my back to the man who, it's clear now that I've rubbed the water from my eyes, is not much more than a boy. I dive into the waves, swimming with an awkward rhythm at first, making little progress. But my strokes become measured as I move beyond the oscillations of the surf into waters so calm that the sky all but dissolves in the sea.

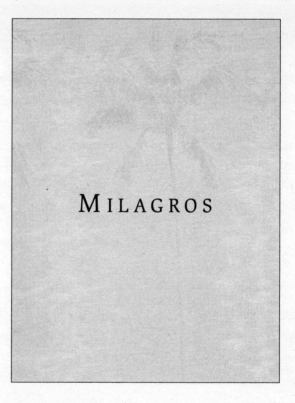

MILAGROS

In the City of the Split Sky

—◊—

Man's like the earth, his hair like grasse is grown,
His veins the rivers are, his heart the stone.
— Wit's Recreations (1640)

My heart is not stone. This river is not my blood. It is not of me, it is other, distinctly so. I sit in the rough-hewn boat, my back to the bow, and watch the milk-brown waters close behind me, where I have been, where I am going, unmarked on this river that cleaves the landscape in two.

We've been travelling for days, my youngest son and I. Montreal, Mexico City, Villahermosa, Palenque, sliding ever deeper into the funnel that is Mexico. At first light this morning, we piled into a van with six others who had signed on for this expedition to unravel the mysteries of the Maya. Our immediate destination: Frontera Corozal, the country's last outpost, that spot on the map where the neatly dotted border is swept to an undulating flow of pink by the Usumacinta. On one side of the river is the dark swath of

Guatemalan forest called the Petén; on the other, the Meseta
de Agua Escondida, Mexico's land of hidden water.

– The English, they are solid. They no fight, they no
passion, exclaimed the boy who'd sat down beside me outside
the museum in Mexico City, begging not money but words.
–Please. Speak English with me.

He dreamed of Australia, he said, if not in this life, then
the next, but he would learn the language now. – Do you
have passion? he asked.

The museum boy's question has fastened like a leech. It
seems to accuse. I want to go back and tell him: Once I felt
everything, so much feeling has left me numb.

A squadron of scarlet macaws strafes the boat, screeching.
My son taps my arm, insists I look, his eyes wide as a child's
although he is already fourteen, but I turn to the birds slowly,
like one of those iguanas, big as crocodiles, that loll, slit-eyed,
in the river mud.

Nothing moves me. I thought when I became single
again (for the first time in my life, really, since I was married
so young) that there would be a great opening up of my
heart, of possibility, of I don't know exactly what. But not
this. I did not expect this drawing in, this shutting out.

Last night, as we drove into Palenque from the airport,
my son struck up conversations with our companions, report-
ing to me their brief biographies: Jim, a young exploration
geologist; James, a retired research chemist who had hiked
the Petén thirty years before; Charlie, a delivery man from
San Diego, a birder intent on adding to his life list; Robert, a
New York decorator making the rounds of Central America's

ruins; Joe, a beach boy from California, our outfitter and cook; and MaryDell, a copper-haired congressman's daughter, an archaeologist and our guide to Yaxchilán, where we will learn to read ancient Mayan stories carved in stone. I am here to write an article for a travel magazine, doing what I can to support myself and my youngest son. He is still too young to stay alone for such a long time. My oldest son, who is eighteen, is with his father. That is how my husband and I settled things, dividing what we shared precisely in half between us. After two years, the pain of this separation remains unbearable, though there is no wound to see. It is a phantom pain, what an amputee must feel, nerves and cells still screaming long after the arm or leg is severed.

My son is proving to be a good traveller. He thrills to all that is new, adjusting to reversals and obstacles as if they were swells in a sea. Not me. It is stasis I crave. There have been so many departures of late: my husband, my oldest son. But, no, I remind myself, it was I who left them. And here I am, leaving again, hoping in the fixity of the unfamiliar to find some respite from change.

The road from Palenque was paved at first but quickly disintegrated to gravel then shrivelled to a narrow track. Through breaks in the fringe of palms and guayacan, I saw *campesinos* with machetes, chopping at the jungle's roots. Trees big as mine shafts smouldered faintly. Sharp-ribbed, chalk-hide cattle nuzzled the swidden pasture, the parchment dewlaps under their chins flapping at wisps of smoke. I sipped at my water bottle as we rode past clearings where brown, naked children played on hardpan courtyards outside thatch-roof

huts. Then the clearings vanished too, and all I saw that
breathed were the brassy butterflies that hovered thick as gnats
over the puddles and chased the fenders of the van as we
splashed through. The road ended abruptly at the river. Only
water flows as deeply into the jungle as we have to go.

All along I tell myself I must observe and record, it is my
job, but I tire quickly of the suffocating vegetation. I yearn
for a simpler landscape, one drawn in straight lines, without
shading, in black and white.

We've been in the boat for hours, heading downstream,
away from the hills where the Usumacinta rises from the
junction of Rió Salinas and Rió de la Pasión. Along the
riverbank, thin paths insinuate themselves into the undergrowth. Just a few years ago, MaryDell tells us, thousands
lived along the river, landless highland Maya resettled into
agricultural co-operatives. But the war in Guatemala has
emptied the settlements; the jungle reclaims the clearings
while the *guerillas* count their dead. Only the *chicleros* and
chateros work along the river now, harvesting sapodilla for
chewing gum and *Chamaedorea* fronds for brides' bouquets.

At the end of one path, a bamboo pole pokes up from the
river mud. Red panties flutter from its tip. The boatman
noses the *lancha* toward the marker and a woman appears, a
small child behind her skirts. We jostle in the boat, tucking
our bundles of clothing, jugs of water and crates of tomatoes,
avocadoes, and pineapples closer under our snakeproof boots
as the woman wades out to the boat, first handing in the
child, then returning to the riverbank to retrieve a cloth
bundle, which she balances on her head, and a brazier, which

she cradles in her arms above the water. The woman settles in silence on the floor, the child nestled between her legs. The boatman pushes off. There are even fewer places now to safely rest the eyes. I turn and watch the red panties until the speck of colour might be mistaken for a lone macaw or the scarlet heart of a bromeliad.

To discourage conversation, I keep my face to the water, to the sky. It is difficult to ignore the incivility of what I do. I sit here in Joe's T-shirt, Charlie's shorts, MaryDell's under-wear, and Jim's socks. Only my boots are my own. Our gear, so carefully selected and stowed, has made a side trip to a city in northern Mexico. It can't possibly catch up with us now. Besides the clothes I had been wearing, all I have that is mine for these ten days in the jungle is my notebook, a camera, and a handbook of Spanish phrases. The trip has barely begun and already I am beholden to strangers, my impulse for order overthrown.

The river bends sharply to the right. The sun spins around to face us. The water, snapping out of its languor, swirls around limestone boulders, eddying green as if another jungle, the twin of what we see, lurks underneath. A mangrove swallow swoops across our bow. Blackbirds scramble amongst the stones. Straight ahead, the riverbank rises sharply, a sheer face lined with half-naked men, fifty of them at least, maybe a hundred, or more, leaning against the gumbo-limbo trees, slouching, hands on hips, sitting on the ledges, legs dangling over the pale, dusty cliff, a scene from *Apocalypse Now*.

We manoeuvre between the rocks, through the aquamarine purl, past small, beached dugouts and knots of women, thigh-deep in the surging water, skirts hoisted brightly to their waists, their hands clutching wads of cloth against crude wooden scrub-boards. Every eye is on us, but no one smiles, no one speaks, no one moves.

Our boat scrapes against stone. The breeze that discreetly fanned us on the water abandons us now. The heat sidles in close.

—You all stay here now while I check this out, says Joe, leaping off the bow of the boat. He stands on the shore, his hand to his eyes as he squints up at the galleries of men, then he breaks into a full-armed wave, — *¡Hola! ¡Gonzalo!*

One of the small, black-eyed men breaks rank and scrambles down the bank toward Joe. Their hand-clasp is the signal. We fumble out of the boat and drag our gear across the rocky strand laid bare by the dry season's extended drought.

The cliff face is daunting. Robert and Jim position themselves at either end of an oversized cooler. Before they can bend to lift it, one of the men runs down the path, tearing from an overhanging tree a long, wide leaf that he puts on like an epaulette. Without a word, he shoulders the cooler in a single heave, swaying lightly to regain his balance, then he trots barefoot up the slope, grinning widely to his friends.

We pitch our tents in a fig grove on the plateau immediately above the riverbank, a respectful distance from the workers' *palapas*, wall-less, palm-thatch huts strung inside with a cat's cradle of hammocks in yellow, red, and blue. Donkeys graze in the long, narrow clearing beside our camp. My son and I set our tent to face southeast, hoping to catch the sunrise between the flaps. The others face theirs into the grove, toward the river or the highlands beyond the Petén, all of us contriving privacy, though we are barely out of reach.

The night is a dark curtain yanked down. I leave my son to prepare for bed and wander a short distance into the clearing, which I see now is an abandoned airstrip lined with heaps of stones, the remains of old signal fires. From the workers' cantina across the way drift accordion strains of *ranchero* songs and, now and then, a mournful *balada*. In recent years I've avoided music with words, especially songs about love and loss. Instead, I listen to Mozart and Bach, choosing sonatas and symphonies that have no personal associations except for the sweet memory of my older son learning to play his piano. The stories in these Mexican songs are unknown to me, but even the melodies tell a tale I'd rather not hear. I wait for my son's breathing to take on the deep, even rhythms of sleep, then I crawl into the tent.

Abruptly, the lights of the cantina extinguish, the music stops. The sounds of the jungle repossess the night. Intermittent thrips and whines. Low, nasal calls that echo through the understorey, rustle and slither past the tent. My weary mind accommodates them all. They are not so unlike the frogs and owls and porcupines in the place I once called home. But some time before dawn, anguished cries pierce the higher air, casting my dreams with tortured children, mothers forced to look, babies flayed alive at the gates of hell.

−Howler monkeys, MaryDell explains to us in the morning.

We've been up since five-thirty when the workers' generator kicked on. Before the sun has cleared the trees, we are sitting with MaryDell, sipping Gatorade and eating mango pancakes.

− The Maya have a story about how those monkeys evolved, MaryDell continues. − One day, they say, the first grandmother was walking with her grandchildren in the forest. The little boy and girl saw a beehive and without asking permission they climbed the tree to get the honey. Well, the grandmother waited for a while, then she called for them to come down. They pretended not to hear. Finally she shouted at them, 'Come down or you'll stay in the trees forever!' But they only made faces at her, climbed higher, and laughed. 'If that's the way you want it,' she said, and she hit the tree four times on each side of the trunk with her cane. Suddenly, the tree grew and grew. It was so tall that the children couldn't climb down even if they wanted to. 'From now on, you'll eat nothing but honey and fruit and your faces will change so I don't recognize you,' she said. And, with that, the grandmother walked away, leaving the small hairy beasts, with their faces that looked almost human, hanging from the branches by their newly grown tails, calling after her in voices that sounded for all the world like the cries of little children.

− The Maya still tell their kids that story, MaryDell concludes, her eye on my son who is swinging Tarzan-like from a liana vine. −To make them obey.

The morning mist has not yet risen but already the lowland heat has pressed dark stains under my arms and breasts, at my waist, between my legs, making me conscious, suddenly, of what an extravagantly creased and folded apparatus this human anatomy is. I sip diligently at my water bottle and, with the others, follow Gonzalo down the path toward the ancient city of Yaxchilán. Gonzalo is not one of the workers hired to excavate the ruins. He's a *vigilante*, paid to protect the site. No one enters Yaxchilán except with him. He has been a guard here for two years, according to Charlie, who quickly befriended the man. Every second month, Gonzalo leaves his thatched hut at the end of the airstrip to spend two weeks in Palenque with his wife and children. In the summer, his son and two daughters stay with him here. This is separation of another sort, I think, made legitimate by necessity. I could abide this, too, for it implies no breach of faith.

My son runs ahead to join Gonzalo and Charlie, who is flipping through his field guide, pointing to this bird and that, anxious for Gonzalo to tell him which ones he might see. He is almost as tall as Charlie. Both tower over the Mexican. I've rarely seen my son at such remove, and I am taken aback by his body, more man than child now, although he still holds his face sweetly open, his need and his desires so generously revealed that I avert my eyes.

The moment we step beyond the clearing, the jungle closes around us, over us too, for the canopy of branches that soars far above us is as solid as a roof. Thick pillars of cedar and mahogany rise, arched with liana vines, roots flaring like webbed buttresses. Bromeliads and epiphytic orchids ornament every limb. The light is green, as if filtered through jade. *Yax* is the Mayan word for green. I've read that the American who first photographed these ruins named the place for the river's green stones. I would have named it for the light.

Under a clearing in the canopy, a limestone wall rises in steps, dripping with wild begonia, philodendron, hibiscus, and canna. I make a note: "Rivals the gardens of Babylon." Gonzalo stops at the far end of the wall, by a stone doorway all but hidden in the extravagant foliage.

This is *El Laberinto*. The Labyrinth. It is the back door to Yaxchilán. Single file, we pass through. Instinctively, I draw a deep breath as I step blindly into the gloom. Those in front find their flashlights, beam them back to me. Bats, startled by the sudden light, palpitate my shoulders, brush my cheeks with claw-tipped wings as they reel to darker sanctums. I swallow my screams for the sake of my son, who points with delight to the cockroaches, big as mice, that scuttle across the toes of our boots.

The passageway is so narrow my elbows scrape the walls. It twists and turns, opens into a vaulted chamber, veers off again, leading down, deeper underground. We move past niches with wide benches set in the masonry, walls limned with plaster, smudged here and there with faint scarlet and royal blue. I find it difficult to breathe. Figures take shape on the walls; MaryDell stops in front of them, speaks to us of visions and blood-letting rites. I must have air. I squeeze past the others and press on ahead, down the corridor, slipping on the damp stones, alone, no clear way out. The passage twists again, up some steps, and then a shard of brilliance, light, and there it is: the main plaza of the city of Yaxchilán.

I move beyond the shadow of *El Laberinto* and wait for the others, struggling to smooth the ragged edges of my breaths. I should have asked if there were another way into the ruins. Ever since I was a child, I cannot bear to be confined. I have always felt smothered when enclosed, not just by walls but also by endless space. Now that I am on my own, constraint especially unnerves me.

It doesn't help to dwell on it, I tell myself.

I shoulder my day pack and walk briskly into the white light. At the centre of the plaza grows a ceiba, the sacred tree of the Maya. It must be ancient. From its enormous trunk, branches rise like outstretched arms toward the sky.

– The roots, they say, reach into Xib'alb'a, the Mayan underworld, says MaryDell, coming up behind me, putting her hand on my shoulder. – Are you okay?

I nod. Since I am the only other woman on the trip, MaryDell seeks out my company, but I am not looking for a friend. When the others join us by the tree, I move to stand by my son.

– At the end of the day, according to Mayan belief, Xib'alb'a rotates above the earth and becomes the night sky, she explains after the group is assembled. – The trunk of the tree is the axis or the Middleworld, the place where we live. The Maya have no heaven or hell, no past or future either, just an Otherworld, a second existence, complete with birds and trees and temples, that mirrors and surrounds the world we inhabit. That's where we were before we were born, and that's where we'll return to when we die. The Otherworld can be entered now too, but only through a trance induced by pain.

I think of the maple trees at home spreading their red leaves on the grass every autumn, as if burying their heads in the earth, their bare branches thrust into the air like roots. But in the north, we take no meaning from such things.

Stone temples line the main avenue of Yaxchilán. Dozens more terrace the hillside that rises from the river. On the summit, three acropoli overlook the site.

MaryDell leads us through one structure after another, teaching us to decipher the neatly boxed columns of symbols decorating lintels, steps, altars, and stelae, the tree-stones that rise like grave markers throughout the ruined city.

A penis draped over a jaguar's head, a serpent coiled across two globes, a king vulture compressed and squared: I resist the notion that these hieroglyphs can be read like words. It is the pictures that draw my eye. Large, intricately chiselled figures fill the spaces between the rows of hieroglyphs like illustrations in a child's storybook: a young man wearing a kilt of jaguar tails and, above his haughty profile, a towering headdress of quetzal plumes; behind him, a woman carrying a bundle tied with a large knot.

– Bird Jaguar IV, he of the twenty captives, translates James, who already reads the glyphs as if they were nothing more than an ornate Central American dialect. – And that's his wife, Lady Great-Skull-Zero.

– And those are blood-letting tools in her hands, MaryDell adds.

As we move from stela to stela, their story unfolds. With a stingray's spine, Bird-Jaguar pierces the tongue of his mother, Lady Evening-Star, who is also called "the woman who lets blood in the dark." She pulls a rope through her tongue, dripping blood into a bowl she clutches to her chest. Bird-Jaguar pierces his wife's tongue too, then he kneels before his mother and slashes the skin of his penis three times, pushing a roll of paper through each wound to absorb the blood. Entranced with pain, he burns their blood, and in the black smoke that rises above their half-closed eyes, the Serpent Path to the Otherworld opens, all the gods of the real and mythic past revealed by the sacrifice of the mother, the wife, the son.

If these were words on a page, I could skim over them lightly or set them aside until I was ready, but I cannot avoid these grim pictures, this story that passes directly to me from the hand of the Maya who carved it a thousand years ago. I press my palm against my lips, as if to guard my own tongue.

This man demands too much, I think. What is his wound, after all, a shallow incision in a fold of skin, compared to the wound of silence he inflicts.

The rhythm of our days is set. The workers' generator and the smell of frying tortillas rouses us before dawn. We spend long days in the temples, translating lintels and stelae. In the evenings, we sit around the campfire listening to the thunder that rumbles impotently inside the livid clouds. We talk of vision rites and circular calendars, a Mayan infinity of past and future that robs the present of its moment.

I hardly see my son. He stays with the men, bounding up the steep, narrow steps to the top of each temple with Charlie, crouching beside James to hear the stories of the jaguar kings. In the evenings, he carves images from the stelae into a walking stick for Robert, who is bothered by arthritis in his knees. He reproduces the emblems for Penis-Jaguar, Bird-Jaguar, and Bird-Jaguar's son. I want to ask him what he thinks of all this, the Otherworld, the pain-induced visions, and the letting of blood, but such a conversation cannot help but speak of relations between husbands and wives, and so I say nothing.

After lunch, we wait out the afternoon heat in the quiet pools at the river's edge, which shrink a little more each day that the drought persists. Beyond the pools, the river bottom drops off sharply. We joke about swimming to Guatemala, to the huge ceiba tree that rises in the centre of the clearing on the other side.

– That's Centro Campesino. It's abandoned now, but it used to be one of the largest of the river co-operatives, says MaryDell, who, even when we relax, can't seem to resist continuing our lessons. – In Bird-Jaguar's time, we could have walked across to their camp on a bridge the Maya built right here, the longest in the world at the time.

She waves at a mound of stones, the remains of ancient pylons, still visible above the water.

–The *guerillas* controlled the river up to this point. When the Guatemalan army came, hundreds escaped from Centro Campesino by swimming across to Mexico. A lot of them drowned. There's quite a current here.

The men have abandoned bathing suits. They strip to their underwear or their bare skin to cool in the river, although Robert, who wears a shirt that seems freshly pressed each day, still retires to the shallows at the far end of the beach for his solitary ablutions. I, too, hold myself apart, avert my eyes from the bodies of the men, keep my own fully clothed, even when I lie in the river pools.

— It's easier this way, I tell the others, scrubbing the sweat from my clothes and my skin in one stroke, stretching out on the rocks to dry in the parching sun.

They take my reticence for modesty, perhaps, or for journalistic reserve. They do not know how much even this requires of me, how rigid I have become.

MaryDell has saved the three acropoli for last. The time has passed so quickly. I smile a little when I say this to the others, for I am aware how certainly this insistence on marking moments marks me too.

Inside the tallest temple on the highest crest above Yaxchilán, we find remains of offerings: maize, a few flower stems, the dust of ashes. It is almost June 21, the longest day of the year, when the sun begins its slow withdrawal. Like the Maya, I always take note of this turning point, a reminder that, even though the heat of summer still lies ahead, the light is slowly giving way to darkness.

The temple was built so that it faces, square-on, the sun as it rises on the morning of the summer solstice. On that one day of the year the sun seems to emerge through a deep cleft in the highlands, which I can see silhouetted against the horizon. I resolve to get up early the next day, our last, and come here alone to witness what the ancient priests saw, what gives this place its Mayan name, the City of the Split Sky.

We sit cross-legged on the temple's crenellated roof-comb. Above us, two king vultures gyre so near that I can make out their white bellies, the blood-red ruffs at their throats.

MaryDell leans over to me. —Do you know why they eat only the dead?

I don't respond. There's no need, for I know she will tell me anyway. My notebook is already fat with her myths and legends, which she repeats with an air of significance that is puzzling to me.

—The Maya, like most civilizations, have a story about a Great Flood, although there's no Noah and no ark. In their version, when the rains begin, two of every species in the world hide themselves in a house on top of a hill, the only place on earth that stays dry. When the rain stops, the animals send a vulture to find out if it's safe to leave the hilltop. The vulture flies in great circles farther and farther away. He's desperately hungry, of course. The Flood has lasted a very long time. When he sees all the drowned animals washed up on the land, the vulture forgets about his mission and drops down to devour the corpses. After he's had his fill, he flies back to the hilltop, but he smells so putrid that the animals won't let him in. They know what he's done. To punish him, they condemn him to live forever on the rotting flesh of the dead. And so, ever since then, vultures circle the sky, watching for the dead and dying, cleansing the world of decay.

I do not know what to take from these stories that fix a creature's destiny in some long-ago act of disobedience. Refusing to come down from a honey-tree, stopping to eat instead of flying straight home: these seem to me to be indulgences, minor crimes at most, certainly not serious enough to warrant punishments that endure to the end of time. I try to take them to heart, as MaryDell seems to intend, but what rule could I have flaunted, what unintended insubordination might have brought me to where I find myself: alone, separated from one son, responsible for this other who is about to become a man.

The jungle stretches below me, a dark undulating sea that flows unbroken to the horizon. MaryDell is saying that ten million people once lived in these lowlands, that Yaxchilán was once a city of fifty thousand or more, that once we could have looked down from this temple onto Bird-Jaguar's plaza and in the distance seen the glint of sixty other cities, a forest of kings.

I try to imagine this other time, but I am too overwhelmed by the present to contemplate a different past. The sea of trees is too much for me. Mumbling excuses, I pick up my day pack and hurry down the back of the temple where tree roots entwine the stone, holding the structure together as they break it apart. The descent is dizzying. Hundreds of tall, narrow steps slope toward the ground. I inch my way sideways down the incline. The sun is already low in the sky. Soon night will drop swiftly, as it does in this place. Alarmed,

I move a little faster. My feet slip on the moss. I fall backward, slamming into the limestone, bumping down several steps before my foot finds a hold.

I don't realize until I am back in camp that the fall has left a deep cut in the skin at my elbow. My camera is smeared with blood. Dried rivulets stripe my leg; blood has drained into my boot, drenching my sock red. I wash it off in the river, but Gonzalo, who has followed me back, insists on ministering to my wound. He carefully picks out bits of stone and pours peroxide over the gash, crooking my elbow to make the flesh gape.

– *¿Le duele?* he asks.

I shake my head. It doesn't hurt at all. He scours the underbrush at the edge of the clearing and comes back with a leaf, which he crushes lightly between his fingers. The fragrance reminds me, oddly, of *guaraná*, the fizzy drink my father used to buy me when he took me with him for his regular Saturday lunch at the hotel where we'd lived when we first moved to Brazil.

– *Guaraná?* I ask, for I have since learned that the drink I loved so much as a child is named for a jungle herb that has a certain medicinal effect: a cure for fatigue, and hardness of heart.

Gonzalo shrugs and lays the leaf on my wound, wrapping it firmly in place with a strip of cloth.

I join the others in the shallows, holding my arm at an angle so as not to wet the bandage. My son is swimming farther out. I tilt my head back into the cool water. I shut my eyes against the searing light.

When I open them, my son is gone.

I sit up, panicked. My eyes sweep the river. He was there, I saw him just a moment before, as I had seen his brother, a tiny child in that other river in the north, years and years ago. One minute, there; the next, disappeared, the water closed indifferently over his head. Fear had paralyzed me, strangled the words that rose in my throat. It was his father who dove into the channel, who swooped under our son's little body, raised him choking into the air.

I see an arm rise in the distance. The screams I have swallowed burst out of me now, a wild, wordless cry that ricochets back and forth across the water.

He is already halfway across. The current will drag him under. I can't get to him in time. I'm not strong enough to save him. – Oh god, I sob. Then another wave of panic gathers and I shriek, –No! Come back!

– ¡Vente! ¡Peligro! ¡Vente, hijo!

The shout is from the riverbank. Gonzalo is standing on top of the cliff, his hands cupped around his mouth. His words, low and stern, draw my son to the shore.

– I'm okay, I wasn't that far out, he says, embarrassed by my tears, but I clutch him to me in the shallows, weak with relief, water dripping from our bodies, blackening the river stones.

That evening, as we eat our supper around the campfire, the air falls still. One deep-throated rumble, and the sky cracks, unleashing months of rain. My son and I dive for our tent.

The wind revives, scoops up the torrent, dashes it sideways against the nylon. We sit back to back, holding up the roof with our hands, staying the corners of the tent with our feet. Through the slash of the storm we hear explosions in the jungle as limbs snap from trees and hurtle to the ground. I rub my head against my son's, murmur reassuring words. Lightning flashes, then a deep tearing sound nearby, and something collapses the tent against my legs. We start to giggle at the futility of sustaining this frail tissue against such a deluge, our laugh becoming hysterical as we imagine this end for ourselves, pummelled to death by rain on our last night amidst ruins that have survived a millennium.

Some time later, the rain lets up long enough for us to clear away the fallen branch and bend the tent pole straight, but the storm revisits again and again in the night, washing through my dreams.

Early the next morning we hear the howler monkeys as if they are directly overhead. Their heart-rending cries cut through the mist, punctuated now by deep-throated snuffles. Charlie taps on the side of our tent.

—Want to come look for howlers?

The clouds are too low. I won't be able to see the sun rise from the temple; I'll have to abandon the private excursion I'd planned. —Sure, I say. —Just give me a minute.

Gonzalo is waiting for us at the edge of the clearing. He wears his usual uniform despite the dramatic change in weather: white embroidered shirt, sagging trousers, brown plastic flip-flops. We follow him down the airstrip, wait while he goes into his hut. He comes out holding a rifle.

–¿*Porque?* Charlie asks. Gonzalo takes the bird book from Charlie's hand and locates the picture of a plump, pheasant-like bird with a crest of feathers above its curved bill.

–Good god, exclaims Charlie, it's a great curassow. They're practically extinct!

– ¡*Es bueno para comer!* Gonzalo runs his tongue along his lips, rubs his belly, and smiles as if he can taste it already.

– *Pero, pronto*, Charlie stammers, trying to find the right foreign words. – *Todos desaparecidos*.

He waves his arm at the forest, trying to conjure emptiness. Gonzalo sees the concern on our faces. My son must look particularly appalled, for Gonzalo pats his shoulder and speaks to him earnestly. I ask Charlie to translate.

– He said, 'Yes, it's true, they disappear deeper into the forest, but don't worry,' he says, 'I'm a good hunter. I can still find them.'

The gun loose in the crook of his fingers, Gonzalo walks ahead of us into the forest. Through the long, drawn-out drought, the jungle didn't die; it lay in wait for the rain to bring it back to life. Now the air is liquid with its scent. Lungs alone seem insufficient to breathe. The forest is like a creature we have stumbled inside. It writhes around us, whispering and heaving, clattering restlessly.

So entranced am I by the forest's intonations, I don't hear the man approach. He appears like a vision on the path. He is dressed not in jaguar tails and feathers but in a simple white shift that hangs to his knees. He stands in a shaft of light and, by the smooth lean silhouette, I can see that he is naked underneath. His feet are bare. His hair falls to his waist, hair of the whitest blond. He turns to me. His eyes are the bluest blue. He raises a hand and smiles, then runs lightly across the path, disappearing into the undergrowth.

– Lacondón Maya, says Charlie. – MaryDell told me we might see him. He's albino, and one of the few traditional Maya left in this forest. He still uses the temples, she says.

Gonzalo takes no note of the man. He leads us deeper into the forest, pausing to warn us of a termite nest or show us flattened underbrush where a brocket deer passed the night. He points to what he hears, and I see a groove-billed ani, a cinnamon becard, the elusive yellow-billed cacique, red-capped manikins, a raucous flock of collared aracari. When I squat behind an elephant-eared bush to relieve myself, I see a black-crested hummingbird half the size of my baby finger, perching on a flower stem.

Then I hear it, the melancholy triple tremolo of the curassow. By the time I get back to the path, Gonzalo is slipping a shell into the cartridge of his gun. He orders us to stay where we are. I reach out to hold him back. He misunderstands and pats my hand. – *No problema*, he says.

Gonzalo steps between the trees and is immediately out of sight. Without him, we are lost. MaryDell will notice if we don't return soon, but it could take her hours, even days, to locate us. My son moves to stand beside me. I put my arm around his shoulders.

– Don't worry. He'll come back.

A gunshot. For a breath, the forest is silent. I want to tell my son, I resolve to tell him one day soon that there are more endings than beginnings in life, which on the face of it makes no sense, but there is comfort in that too.

When Gonzalo reappears, he shrugs and makes a little flapping motion with his fingers, a bird disappearing in the bush. We are relieved, and would happily have turned back to camp then, but Gonzalo keeps on the trail of the monkeys. I can hear them. We are following their unearthly shrieks deeper and deeper into the forest, over great fallen cedars, past freshly sprouted waterfalls. Finally, Gonzalo stops. He puts a finger to his lips to silence us, then mouths a raspy, low-pitched *Humpphh . . . humpphh*. We don't move. My neck grows stiff with staring into the upper reaches of the canopy. *Humpphh . . . humpphh*. The incongruous grunts burst at regular intervals from Gonzalo's slight frame. Then the real thing, close by. *Humpphh. Humpphh.*

Gonzalo veers down a gully torn in the forest by a falling tree, climbs a short limestone cliff, and crouches, calling encouragement to us as we scramble to mimic his stealth. When we finally reach his side, he points straight up, and there, high overhead in the topmost tangle, are one, two, five howler monkeys.

They know we're here. Three small ones climb hand over hand down a liana vine to get a better look. An enormous female swings by her tail onto a nearby branch, whooping herself into a frantic howl. The babies move in closer, positioning themselves directly overhead.

I cannot believe our good luck. I pull out my camera. The baby monkeys grin down and let loose a stream of urine and faeces on our heads. We yowl and dive for cover as they scramble back into the treetops, the adults roaring their approval, the babies laughing hysterically.

By the time we return to camp, the others have struck the tents and are preparing to leave. We hurriedly pack our gear and stow it in the boat, scanning the cliff face for Gonzalo. We left him at his hut, thinking he would follow as soon as he put away his gun.

The *lancha* is about to push off when Gonzalo finally appears, running down the path. He holds out a gift for my son: two scalps of curling feathers, one glossy black, the other peppered black and white. The matched crests of a male and female curassow.

My son hesitates. Gonzalo urges the birdskins on him. Then they both turn to me.

– *Gracias, muy amable*, I say.

As my son takes the crests, Gonzalo shakes my hand. It is not the handshake I've always known but the double clasp I've seen here, between friends.

As we round the oxbow, heading back toward Frontera Corozal, we can see Gonzalo still standing at the top of the cliff, waving. My son leans against me, strokes the feathered crests against his cheek as he used to rub the baby blanket my mother crocheted for him, a child always drawn to softness, just as my other son prefers the edge. I know them both better than I know myself. What I feel for them can never be diminished, whatever the distance. I look ahead at the milk-green river, a rend in the jungle that thrusts wildly from either side, conspiring to entwine, to scar over this wound.

SONG OF THE JAPANESE WHITE-EYE

—⁓—

The birds rise up around the bed, their great wings heaving, undulating in slow motion so that the light shafting from the skylight they fly toward glints off their feathers, iridescent, obsidian.

—Wake up! I whisper, nudging the man who sleeps beside me.

But his eyes remain closed. The miracle is mine. These elegant, enormous birds, rising to the light: what can they be? Black as ravens, but larger, immense and lovely, splendidly black, like jet or the fur of panthers.

I sit up in the bed, marvelling at the birds, breathless at their beauty, not concerned with how they came to be here, only honoured by their presence, for creatures this magnificent must surely be rare; but lamenting, too, for they are leaving, disappearing one after the other through the square-cut hole in the ceiling directly above my head.

Then one dips its wings and, without turning, drifts effortlessly down, settling on the floor. The others follow, one by one, dropping back into the room without a sound. And I am so happy, so grateful that they have returned, until I notice the small animals gripped in their talons, headless furred creatures, matted with blood. The birds dart their beaks into the bodies, tearing at the flesh. It comes to me with a shock, they are ruthless scavengers, and they crowd closer around my bed, entrails glistening at their throats, their sly black eyes fixed on mine.

—I had the strangest dream last night, I say to my lover as we walk across the hotel lawn, which is dappled with peacocks, golden plovers, and zebra doves.

We are heading for a path we noticed yesterday when we arrived. It curves into the slope of sugar cane that stretches toward the Sleeping Giant, the looming volcanic backdrop to the beaches on this side of Kauai. My lover is in Hawaii for a five-day Arctic conference, and although I don't share his affection for that cold, featureless place, I can never satisfy my lust for sun, and so I have come along. Scientific matters, contaminant flow to uninhabited places, the warmth of water deep under the ice, occupy his days and most evenings too, but in the mornings, before breakfast, we have an hour to ourselves, which we spend with our binoculars, looking for birds.

—I dreamt about birds, I say. —Huge birds, some species I've never seen before. They were unbelievably beautiful, the colour of ravens but enormous, like ospreys. At first they seemed to be flying away, but then they were landing and, when they perched around the bed, I saw that they were actually quite ugly, grotesque, like gargoyles, and they were ripping apart these animals they held in their claws, eyeing me as if I'd be next.

I pause.

– The odd thing was, I wasn't scared. Mostly, I was annoyed, not at them but at myself, for making a mistake like that, not noticing from the beginning how loathsome they really were.

My lover keeps his eyes on the distance as we walk. Now he stops, lifts his glasses, and says abruptly, – Up there, in that tree.

–Where?

I lift my binoculars and I'm sucked swiftly into the land-scape, into the tree, now a snare of branches, which I scan. –I don't see it. Damn, we need a system. Are you looking at the palm beyond the sugar cane at, say, two o'clock? Or that round little tree with the red berries at ten o'clock?

–The small one. Looks like a cardinal. There. It's moving down now. It's near that vine with the orange flowers. It's a new one for me. Looks like a cardinal, except it's grey and white, with a red head.

I see it now too. He searches through the pocketsize bird book we picked up at the airport, looking for a likeness, but I'd have recognized this one anywhere. Its wings are swept back like a morning coat from the white-silk body, and it has a thick bill the colour of burnished pewter, as if that part alone was wiped clean after its head was dipped in blood.

– Red-crested cardinal. Definitely, he says, waving the book at me. – Look, it's also called the Brazilian cardinal.

He jots the place and date of the sighting in the margin. I keep my glasses focused on the cardinal, watch it poke about the flamboyant flower clusters. I wait for the flood of warmth that always envelopes me in a tropical landscape. A peculiar feeling that tells me I've come home, even though for years now I've lived in the north. The palms at the airport, the poinsettia hedge along the road, the cuticles of beach we passed as we drove to the hotel: none of it, not even the sight of this bird from my childhood, has touched me as I expected it would.

The dream has disgruntled me. Those birds! Their treacherous beauty, those vulture eyes come to mind more clearly than if the creatures had actually been in our room. I awoke this morning weighted with disappointment that bordered on despair. The birds did not alter. They had been monstrous all along. It was I who hadn't seen.

– Let's go back, I say. – I feel quite chilled.

My lover takes my hand. – It's icy! You're such a lizard, he teases, folding both my hands in his and blowing on them with his sweet, warm breath, covering my hands, my neck, my lips with kisses.

Sometimes he says I'm a snake; and he's right, at times my blood runs so cold it hardly seems to flow at all. I'll feel my hand turn frigid, look down, and there it is, a corpse's claw, white as death, the nail of one finger or another a purplish blue. This no longer alarms me, although it is unsettling, for when I move that finger I feel nothing, as if it's no longer part of me.

Back in the hotel, I run hot water in the sink and spread my hands in the heat. Magnified under water, they puff bright pink, all but the third finger on my left hand, which stays shrunken and white.

—Perhaps the dream was a sign, I say. —Maybe we should call the wedding off.

—No way, he says, massaging the Lazarus finger back to life.

It takes so long. The point comes, as it always does, when I think: What if this time the blood doesn't start to flow? What if all my fingers, one by one, drain white, then my hands, my arms and legs, until I am nothing but a torso and this too-faintly beating heart?

Perhaps my lover is right, and I am a lizard-woman, a *kupua*, the Hawaiian chimera that takes two forms, lizard and human, one to devour, one to charm. Though it can't be so, for in the stories I've read, the treacherous two-bodied creature, *kupua*, is always a man.

The wind here never stops. The palm trees lean with it, scratch their fronds against the ground. Clouds scuttle endlessly. The hotel trembles with the heavy oscillation of the waves. Nothing is still. The leaves on the bushes, the ocean as far as the eye can see, everything flickers restlessly. The constant agitation is disquieting. I stay inside, where the windows face away from the sea, and try to loosen my mood, let the heat, at least, work its familiar magic on me.

Our room is on the third floor. It has no balcony, and yet as I lie on the bed trying to read, I hear a commotion right outside the window. I move the curtain. A sable wing, flashing white, brushes so close I recoil. A mynah has built a jumbled twig nest under the eave. She watches me, unblinking, her black eye fierce in its brilliant yellow setting.

Below, the flowers on the frangipani that border the swimming pool release their sweet fragrance to the air. Frangipani is the British name. To the Hawaiians, it is the graveyard tree, for that is where the British settlers planted it, a redolent ring around their dead, sweeter than roses, less susceptible to heat and this relentless breeze. Or maybe they call it the graveyard tree because it flowers when it seems most dead. The whorls of white petals are so incongruous on the gnarled, leafless stems that it occurs to me the hotel staff has pinned them there to make this place seem more hospitable, the beguiling paradise it is supposed to be.

I stand by the window ledge until the mynah's mate returns. The two birds rub their heads together, they stroke each other's beaks, and they make such loving noises that, for no apparent reason, I begin to weep.

I must pull myself together. It is true, I have been ill for many months with a persistent inflammation in my lungs that leaves me exhausted, discouraged at my body's frailty. I am counting on this holiday to recover my health.

I spend the rest of the morning lying on the bed reading about Kauai. It is the oldest of Hawaii's islands, the first volcano in the underwater chain to push its lava up above the sea. It was also the first discovered by the Polynesians who installed their king at the mouth of the Wailua River, which I can see from our room. Generation after generation, Polynesian queens returned to this place, to the *heima*, the sacred birthing temple, where the royal heir was born. To announce each birth, they beat on hollow river rocks that they called bell stones.

The stories invigorate me. In the afternoon, I leave the tourist women giggling in the hotel lobby in their fake-grass skirts as they try to mime with fluttering hands the song that whines from the ghetto blaster on the floor. I walk along the highway toward the Wailua River, my steps in pleasing rhythm with the jingling of the silver bracelet I wear on my ankle to gentle my pace. My friend Sharon gave it to me in the last days of my marriage, after I confessed to her the image that came to mind when I thought of myself: a bloodied carcass on the highway, indistinct and flayed, nothing left but glistening bone and sinew.

—Wear this, she said, to remember who you are.

The landscape I am passing through seems oddly familiar. Of course, I realize, I've seen it all before. *South Pacific*, *Blue Hawaii*, all the great South Sea romances were filmed here on the Coconut Coast. I can't help myself, I hum a few bars of "Some Enchanted Evening," and the words of all the verses come back to me. Once, I took the lyrics of such songs to heart, trusted in a soul's single destiny, one man for all eternity, but such romance requires more innocence than I can muster now.

No Polynesian palace stands at the mouth of the sacred Wailua, only the Coco Palms Hotel. Its balconies hang in mid-air and one wall is collapsed, exposing toilets and curtains that flap at windows boarded up against the hurricane that blew across the island three years ago, stripping sand from the beaches and toppling even the pliant palms.

I follow the river inland. Along the bank, a black-crowned night-heron poses as a reed. Its feathers glint in the sun. The bird dips in the water, spears a fish, flips it in the air, and swallows it whole, shivering with satisfaction as it bends to preen. But the dream birds have made me wary of pleasure: I feel the anguish of the fish.

I used to do this as a matter of course, train my eye to the darker side. Even a black heart can smile, I'd repeat under my breath, a mantra against my Pollyanna self. I taught myself to scrutinize every kindness for hidden malice, examine compliments for artfully concealed slights. Where there was harmony, I listened for notes of bitterness, and when someone offered friendship, I considered first the price. In the Saviour himself, I could have found faults.

Ever since my marriage ended seven years ago, I have practised the art of seeing shadows, until I am no longer dazzled by surfaces and I see the shape of the soul close underneath a human face. Even with the man I am about to marry, I am not blind. I count his shortcomings among his merits. I love him for all that he is.

I have taken the bus to Ka'apa to find the real Hawaii and its people: the plump, broad-faced Polynesians; a market, perhaps, or a restaurant where I can sample the true taste of this place instead of the hamburgers and beefsteaks that announce more clearly than the road signs that this is an American state.

I've been told there is a farmers' market, but when I find the scattering of pickup trucks, they offer only the familiar grocery-store varieties of wilted lettuce, radishes, and a few oranges and limes. I ask for pineapple, passion fruit, tamarinds, and taro. I've been longing for the taste of pineapple grown in iron-red soil and freshly harvested, sliced open with a machete at the curb, like the ones my mother allowed us at the end of a day of shopping when I was a little girl in Brazil.

– The pineapple's all grown for export, the vendor tells me. – Anyways, it's not native to the islands either.

Weary and empty-handed, I walk back to the edge of town, to the convenience store where the bus driver told me he picks up passengers on his return. A man dressed in knee-high black boots, white pants, and an open shirt is sitting on the curb. From a distance, he looks pleasingly tropical, but as I come closer, I see he is dishevelled, the pants stained at the crotch and torn, the shirt buttonless, and the rubber boots too big, incongruous in the heat. I wander back the way I came, scanning the road for the bus. When I return, the man is gone. I take his place, though as soon as I settle myself on the curb, he reappears before me. I think he is staring at me, for his head is inclined in my direction, but he wears sunglasses with deep-orange lenses, so I cannot tell for certain.

– Did I take your seat? I ask.

He shakes his head and smiles. His teeth are misshapen, forcing his mouth to a grimace. He moves one step to the left. Now he is directly in front of me, and I realize with a start that he is not looking at me but up the flared leg openings of my shorts. I jump up and walk into the little store.

–What time is the bus due?

–Don't know.

–Did I just miss one? I've been waiting at least half an hour.

–Don't know. Wasn't watching.

–How often do the buses come?

–Hard to say.

The clerk is more disinterested than rude. I scan the shelves for something distinctively Hawaiian, pay for a bottle of coconut syrup, and return to the curb. The man is no longer there. I debate with myself for a moment, then sit down and dip my fingers into the syrup, sucking on the cloying sweetness. I decide to flag a taxi, but none appears.

An hour passes, and still the bus does not come. I consider walking back along the highway but I am already exhausted by this excursion and night will soon fall, abruptly, as it does so near the equator. I could call my lover. But no, I have forsworn such dependencies. Asking for help risks being let down or, worse, it means putting yourself under someone else's thumb.

The dishevelled man returns, stumble-walking down the road. He sits beside me on the narrow curb, then sidles close so his leg rubs against mine. I cross to the public telephone on the other side of the road.

Please be there, I chant under my breath as the desk clerk rings first our room, then the conference hall, finally paging him over the intercom. But he cannot be found.

I leave a message that I'll be on the highway, please come for me. Then I hang up.

My hand on the heavy black receiver, the stifling telephone booth, my overbearing need, something triggers a memory of hanging up a different public telephone. And hard on this, another, more powerful recollection. Watching nighthawks dip and the daylight drain from the autumn sky, I admit to my husband how much I'd yearned to hear his voice when I'd made that call from the hospital, and he tells me that the messages I'd left all over Europe had reached him, in fact, but after trying once to call me back, he'd given up because he knew I'd be all right, I always was.

But I hadn't been. For hours I had stood at the pay telephone near the intensive care unit, desperate to locate him, calling everyone I could think of, even government embassies. As my mother lay unconscious and my sisters knelt praying, I needed my husband. No one else in the world, I thought, shared my convictions but him.

I had always put the beginning of the end later. But no, it was on that October night, the one that comes back to me. Then, I had swallowed and said nothing. Now, my cheeks sting as if I've been slapped.

I think of the years it took to recognize the litter of broken confidences, the trail of signs that should have warned me that this man could not be counted on, that he'd always give too little, want too much, and in the end never want me, and me alone, enough. The years it took to forgive my husband who, even as he withheld it, let me glimpse the life I desired. But I cannot yet forgive myself, or make myself believe that I won't let it happen again.

I close the door to the telephone booth and set out down the highway. That was another life, I tell myself sternly. I am a different woman now, and this, an altogether different man.

On our last day on Kauai, my lover and I rent a car. We plan to tour the island to see the sights, especially what the guide-book calls "The Grand Canyon of the Pacific."

I've always thought I liked islands. My great-uncle Des, a bachelor travelling salesman who sold lingerie door to door in the north during the Depression, owned an island in the lake district of Ontario, which he left to my father and his brothers, who got rid of it for next to nothing. I resented that, even though it happened long before I was born. I imagined I would have lived there, all the landscape I loved within sight and neatly circumscribed. But now that I'm on an island, I see it differently. I am three thousand miles from everywhere, surrounded, hemmed in by restless waves.

I think this as we drive along the highway that traces the rim of Kauai all the way to the corrugated mountains of the Na Pali coast. We stop first at the road's northern limit, at a beach famous for surfers, but the wind is whipping the waves to colossal curls and so we are entirely alone. We leave the beach and explore a nearby cave, a stone vault with a low, narrow passage that leads to a smaller chamber beyond.

A curtain of wild morning glories filters daylight on the far side, although when I push aside the vines, I see not ocean but a courtyard open to the sky.

—Must be the remains of one of those lava tubes, my lover says, though I can tell by the tone of his voice that he senses the magic too.

A tangle of shrubs, ferns, and flowers grows in the lava-soil, and even a monkey-pod tree. Other caves open off the courtyard, secret subterranean recesses like the ones I've read about, where Polynesian women gave birth, where families huddled during tropical storms, and where women and children fled when the white men came.

My lover comes up behind me, puts his arms around my waist, pulls me close against him.

—If we want to see the canyon, we'd better press on, he says.

We retrace the rim of the island, driving past the lighthouse on the point, where blue-billed red-footed boobies nest by the hundreds on a cliff, past the valley of the Hanalei River, where we see a black-necked stilt, common moorhens, American coots, and finally, a truly Hawaiian bird, the koloa maoli, which looks disappointingly like a mallard. We sing "Puff the Magic Dragon." My lover knows all the words. We continue to the far limit of the road, to the beach at the mouth of the Waimea, where Captain Cook, the first white man, had set foot, and where he was killed a year later by the same men who in the beginning had called him God.

At last, we turn inland. The peak of the old volcano that is Kauai is the wettest spot on earth, yet the canyon eroded in its western slope is all but desert, steep cliffs of striated red earth and, at the bottom, an oasis traced through with a single silver line, the Waimea River.

My lover is eager to hike down to the river that carved this gorge, though he doesn't insist.

– Are you up to it? he asks gently.

I stall, reading the guidebook. In one place, it states the canyon is 10 miles long; in another, 14. It is either 2,750 or 3,657 feet deep. The discrepancies are disconcerting. On the other hand, the dirt path that meanders past the lip of the canyon looks well trampled. A good sign.

– As long as you don't mind me stopping to rest. Please, if you want to, go on ahead.

– There's no rush, he says, shouldering the day pack and setting off down the path.

I follow, feeling uneasy already that I might not be able to keep up, hoping he doesn't resent the reassurances I seem to need, dreading that he'll come to hate me for this.

We pass through a screen of dense forest and abruptly the terrain turns dry. Stones clatter underfoot. Twisted shrubs and thwarted trees cling desperately to the red rock, which is scratched here and there with shrivelled sedges. We are barely out of sight of the lookout when, at a cliff face, the path stops.

– I guess we go along that ledge, he says, pointing to a jutting shelf of stone barely a foot wide.

The rock sheers away in a drop of at least a hundred feet. I peer down at the treetops. I haven't yet admitted to him one of my peculiarities. When faced with a precipice,

I am overwhelmed by an urge to jump. This is not a fear of falling. That would make sense. In fact, it would be foolish not to be afraid of slipping off this cliff. No, this is something else entirely. A deep desire, a need to leap. —You think you're superwoman, my ex-husband used to tease. —You think you can fly.

Maybe. Or maybe I just want to leave by the fastest route I can. Either way, I know this urge to be not quite sane, and so I keep it to myself.

—I'll check it out, my lover says, and before I can object he is making his way across the ledge, back pressed against the rock, facing the abyss.

I turn away. I can't watch.

—It's easy! he shouts from the other side. —And the path continues over here. Come on!

Come on, come on, come on, his voice echoes across the canyon. The only other sounds are barnyard noises: the bleat of distant goats, crowing cockerels, the grunt of foraging pigs. The forest below is populated with Captain Cook's farm animals gone feral. Their familiar voices lend the scene a bucolic tone, and I am reassured. I step onto the ledge.

—Don't look down. You'll be fine. Just a little farther, five more steps.

And I make it safely across, into his arms.

We aren't even halfway down and already it is mid-afternoon. No one seems to be following in our footsteps. The only signs of human life in the canyon are the tourist helicopters that buzz the gorge every so often, scattering the long-tailed tropicbirds. I check my watch regularly, calculating how long we've been gone, how many hours we might need for the climb out, how soon we should turn back.

We crouch to slide fifty feet or more down a bald hump of red stone, and abruptly the vegetation changes again. Broad-crowned deciduous trees shelter ferns and streams that meander over mossy outcroppings of rock. Except for the snuffling of wild boars, this could be Ontario.

My lover exclaims at the beauty of this place, but it is too inconstant to be attractive to me. The island is a testament to randomness. Every plant and animal is here by chance. Seeds and spores and larvae have all drifted in from other places, floated on the waves or the wind, or in the digestive tract of some passing bird. This explains why there are no snakes or frogs, and the only mammals that were here before humans were bats. The guidebook claims Kauai means "fountainhead of many waters," but I have found another, more fitting translation: "place of things washed ashore." Even the birds are mostly migrants.

A bird that neither one of us recognizes has been piping us into the canyon, flitting from branch to branch just ahead of us along the path, trilling the same lyrical riff in tireless repetition.

—That bird's been following us for a while, he says. —But it keeps moving. I can't get a fix on it.

—Sounds like a warbler.

Even as I say this, I know it can't be so, for nothing here is what it seems. The toothed leaves with square stems, which I swear are mint, have no fragrance at all. The violas, which I recognize from the low-growing borders around my own flower garden, bloom here on shrubs as tall as a man. Shells that belong on beaches live on trees: clusters of ram's horns and tiny pointed whorls cling to the bark, camouflaged as lichens and dead leaves. Although we've yet to hear it, they produce a sound that some describe as a piercing song. – Maybe it's the tree shells, I add.

–Well, according to the book, there's only one warbler in Hawaii and it's not found on Kauai.

The lilting melody accompanies us deeper into the gorge. I relax to its predictable, persistent phrases, as if at last I've found a faithful guide to this chameleon place, which continues to shift and mutate, growing stranger as we approach the canyon floor. The plants have swelled to preposterous proportions. One has leaves as long as hammocks. A twenty-foot flower stalk has toppled across the path. There are plantains too big to hold in my arms, lobelias that tower over our heads. Every shrub aspires to be a tree, every tree drips with gorgeous fruits and flowers in the most unlikely shapes and hues. And always the birdsong drawing us down, down into the gorge.

– Maybe that's not a bird after all, I whisper, though there's no one but him to hear.

Maybe it's the Menehunes, I think, those pygmies who work like Trojans through the night and amuse themselves through the day with bamboo flutes that they play with one nostril, breathing haunting, soothing songs.

We walk slowly, side by side now, hand in hand, dwarfed by the extravagant vegetation, hushed as the phantom bird flits ahead, singing us to the Waimea.

My lover nuzzles my hair, which I no longer cut short or pull back but wear long and wildly curling. Unrepressed, he says. —Let's make love.

—But what if someone is following?

—Over there, across the river, it looks like there's a clearing in the trees.

The riverbed is wide and strewn with boulders, but the river itself doesn't amount to much, just a trickle that stubbornly continues to cut into the bottom of the canyon it has gouged. He jumps across, stone to stone, disappears into the foliage on the other side, then reappears and waves. —It's perfect!

Eddies of water swirl in the gullies between the river stones. I am almost halfway across before I realize I should have taken off my boots. I am more sure-footed without shoes. The water is so clear I can't tell how deep it is. I think that touching the black pebbles will barely wet my fingertips, but my hand plunges into the icy water past my wrist and the stones are still beyond my reach. Two-thirds of the way across, the river reveals itself. What seemed a thin stream from the bank is a surging funnel of water. I look up and down the riverbed for a better place to cross, but the channel widens on either side of me. Even here at its narrowest, it is too wide to jump.

—I can't, I yell across.

—Sure you can. Just a minute, I'll give you a hand.

And he leaps across the stones to the one closest to me and stretches out his arm.

I stretch, too. Our fingers don't quite touch.

—Jump. I'll catch you.

—No!

I look down into the rushing water and I feel that urge again, the urge to leap, not over, but down.

—Just wade across then. Take off your boots. It's not very deep. It's beautiful over here, wait till you see.

He winks. —I'll make it worth your while.

Oh my love, if only you knew how much I want to try. I shake my head.

—I can't.

By the time I make my way back to the riverbank, I have to sit to control my shaking. The warbler is somewhere above me, for I hear its endless song as if it trills inside my head. It must have a nest nearby, I think, and, with tidal force, another memory washes over me, of a warbler's nest I found in our woods in the north, an olive-coloured bird sitting on the tiny woven cup. For hours I crouched in the underbrush, watching her through my binoculars. I wanted to know if her young had hatched, how many there were. I would take the news back to the house, share it with my husband and sons. Finally the warbler flew off, but just as I moved closer to peek into the nest, she returned and I heard squawking from inside. I focused the glasses again. I expected to see three or four tiny hairless creatures, but there was only one, one grotesque featherless skull, one gaping beak. This was no hatchling warbler, it was a cowbird, only a few days old and already as big as its surrogate mother. When the warbler flew off again, I scrabbled in the tall grass under the nest and there they were, three smashed shells, the tiny bodies infested, rotting.

– I'm so sorry, I cry into the arms of my lover, who has rushed across the water to me. – It's not you. It's me. I just can't seem to make sense of anything. All my life I've been like that stupid warbler. Listen to her. If she only knew. Someday a cowbird is going to come along and push her babies out of the nest and lay a giant egg in their place. And the dumb warbler is going to knock herself out nurturing and loving this thing that's been foisted on her. She'll convince herself it's her own. She'll never understand she's been betrayed.

This man who loves me says nothing, but lies back on the grass behind me, lifts his binoculars and scans the treetops. He is still for a long, long time, long enough for me to stop weeping and start feeling foolish for what I've said. When he sits up, he thumbs through the bird book, then passes it to me, holding it open at a certain page.

– Look. It's not a warbler at all. It's a Japanese white-eye. It's a distant relative of the island honeyeaters, those fabulous birds with the long, curved beaks. The ones that are extinct.

He puts his arm around me and draws me backwards onto the grass. Here at the bottom of the canyon, there is no wind. The sun is warm on my skin.

– It's not stupid at all, he says. – It's a survivor. Just listen to it sing.

The Day of the Dead

—◠—

I.

Come, let me show you the village. It isn't very large: two streets draped down the hillside to the river, a few connecting roads that cross. It will take less than an hour and, really, I'd rather not go alone.

This is where I grew up, through the early years until I was in school, then again through adolescence. The charmed hiatus of middle childhood I spent elsewhere, in Brazil. I have claimed other places longer, it's true, but in the end, this is the place I call home. No, not because family lives here still; because here are my dead.

There's not much to it, is there? Hardly more than can be taken in at a glance. If this were Greece or Mexico, it might seem exotic, a few hundred souls clustered together at the river's bend. But this small Ontario village was never poor enough or pretty enough or sufficiently remote for the prophets of progress to pass it by. It has a subdivision now and a quickie mart and a video rental store.

Oh, it's been here quite some time. Two hundred years, they claim, a surprising boast from the offspring of those Scots and Pennsylvania Dutch settlers who held truth so dear. In fact, the land was virgin forest then; the village, a hopeful miller's dream. It did thrive once, though, a century ago. There were stores and several churches and even hotels where the stagecoach to London stopped.

When my mother's mother's people settled out on the Tenth Concession, this was "town." When my great-uncles grew up and left the farm, this was where they came, where they built the planing mill that left them deaf, and where they finally took jobs in the carriage factory, painting gold and silver filigree, thin as half a dozen ermine hairs, on the side panels of surreys and delivery wagons. The carriage factory became Wallbanks' Spring Factory and then The Buggy Works, a weekend antique market where, one day years ago, when my boys were very young, I found a wooden cheese box filled with inlaid ebony dominoes, which I didn't buy, for they cost as much as two weeks' groceries. That same night, the building burned to the ground, and the dominoes, the cruets, the rattan fern stands and ruby glass kerosene lamps, all the frayed quilts and overpriced china figurines that schoolboys, now great-grandfathers, won for their mothers at the fall fair, all of it was turned to ashes, not even worth sifting through, though I tried, there on the corner, where those used cars are parked in rows.

Sometimes I try to see it, this village of mine, through the eyes of a stranger, a young man thinking to buy one of those bungalows lined up like Monopoly pieces in Scott's horse pasture back behind where the brickyard used to be, or maybe a middle-aged woman like myself just passing through on a sunny afternoon drive, looking for quaint rural views to render in watercolour for city living rooms. There's one: the stately red brick with white pillars framed by black, bending pines, though the identical twin houses erected on what was once the front lawn ruin the effect, don't you think?

So much has been converted, made useful in that sensible Scots way. Like that apartment building kitty-corner from us. That's where I started school: P.S. 24. The row of windows on the right, that was Miss Goetz's classroom, grades one and two. I still see the splatter-painted maple leaves taped to the glass, someone's kitchen window now.

Every fall I collected leaves at that corner, first for my mother, then for my teachers, for my oldest sister after she moved west, and finally, as mementoes for myself. I wonder why they cut that red maple down. It bore the biggest, darkest leaves you ever saw. Leaves the colour of carpet in a fine hotel; leaves the colour of dried blood.

This is where I brought Karl, the village veterinarian's son, when I first started to babysit him through all those after-school afternoons. We'd pick the most magnificent leaves, and all the way home we'd play peek-a-boo, hiding behind our scarlet fans like demented courtesans, squishing our faces into goofy glares and grins, then whisking the leaves aside, Surprise! We never stopped the game. Even when he was too old for it and I only babysat after dark, we still played it everywhere. That last night, too, as he held up his arms, his sweater caught around his ears. I pulled it off and there he was, eyes crossed, tongue lolling, and we fell to the floor laughing so hard I thought I'd . . .

Well.

You wouldn't believe it, how fragrant the village was then, especially in the autumn. That wonderful dry-leaf smell, a faint whiff of stewing crabapples and chili sauce drifting from back kitchens, the sharp scent of woodsmoke, an acid tinge of pig manure if the wind was blowing from the east and, every so often, the stink of glue from the sandpaper factory where my father worked. Since then, the closest farms have been surveyed and paved, the wood furnaces exchanged for gas, leaf-burning banned. But the factory survives. Only one kind of industry gives the place its smell now.

I wish I could show you the village I first knew. English's General Store, with barrels of apples on the verandah and, inside, glass jars filled with cookies, a certain flat type crusted in orange crystal sugar, a gingery, chewy confection the taste of which I've never found again. When I lived here, there were two general stores, a bank, a post office, two hardware stores, an appliance shop, butcher shop, fire hall, lumberyard, feed mill, two restaurants, a hairdresser, even a woman of easy virtue, it was said, who lived above one of the stores.

I still see it. The way it was, the way it is, all the stages I witnessed between and some I only imagine: a perpetual becoming. The buildings shape-shift as I pass, each writhing through its own metamorphosis, porches falling away, decks emerging, sheds collapsing, garages rising in their place, clapboard in succession a dozen different hues, the inverted iron V-frame of the swings where I swung and then pushed Karl transmuting to this playground of arsenic-preserved wood.

Do you see that house, the buff-coloured brick? My great-aunt and great-uncle lived there. Every Saturday morning, in the years after we returned from Brazil, my mother, my sisters, and I would clean their house, and the houses of the other great-aunts and great-uncles in the village too. Alice and her girls, that's what they called us. The houses all smelled the same, of overheated stale breath and damp flour in rusting tins. My older sisters and my mother did the kitchens and the bathrooms. I beat the rugs, mopped the floors under the beds, and dusted. That was my favourite job, raising the glass fronts of the Wernicke Elastic Bookcase, running a cloth over the burgundy spines: *Helen of the Old House*, *Pride and Prejudice*, *Mother's Remedies*. I did my work well, polishing the frets under the strings of my great-uncle's mandolin, wiping fingerprints from piano keys, shaking out the antimacassars, winding the adamantine mantel clock and resetting the time, taking care not to bend the hands. I lingered longest at my great-aunts' dressers, where one by one I lifted the French ivory puff box, the nail buffer, and the round hand mirror off the cutwork cloth, the narrow silver tray of amber and tortoise-shell combs, the blown-glass ball with the rose trapped inside, its slender stem hung with garnet and cameo rings. I rubbed Hawes lemon oil into the dark wood, spread a freshly ironed cloth embroidered with pirouetting ballerinas or flower baskets, then returned each cherished object, spotless, to its memorized place.

I made those houses my own with each brush of the dusting cloth. "The Charge of the Light Brigade" is etched line for line in my mind's eye, and underneath that engraving on the sideboard, a gaily painted woodpecker eternally tips toothpicks from its cast-iron log. I've preserved intact the great-aunts and -uncles' houses, and newer ones, too: Karl's house up the hill, past where the sidewalk stops, too modern to have changed much on the outside, but inside, a blue cowboy bedspread is snugged forever under an eight-year-old boy's chin.

You don't see any of this, of course. I apologize. I go on like an old crone, although my own sons have barely come of age. I am not a very good guide, I'm afraid. I walk beside you, but we are walking different streets.

And how crowded they are! I try not to stare at the people who pass, but I always steal a glance, convinced I will recognize the face although I haven't lived here for years. Wasn't she the girl who sat behind me in Miss Goetz's class? Or was she that little friend of Karl's?

Or is she flesh and blood at all? For I see apparitions everywhere. They wander down the river road to swim at the dam, long since gone. They push through wrought-iron gates into the park where the factory now stands, the men waiting with grain sacks, fragrant and freshly emptied for the race, children riding bicycles streaming red and gold crepe. And there, on that lawn, a young woman with mink-black hair and a long, lovely body inside that simple, stylish shift, not from English's store, certainly, nor made on some mother's sewing machine. He comes to her, the young man who lives in that house, the one who taught me to read, not words but the souls of books he brought to me as I babysat Karl in the veterinarian's house up the hill, and he slips his arm around her waist, as if he has done it all his life, and leads her up the stairs to his front door, his back to me, unseeing, though she turns at the last moment and watches me hurry past.

Phantoms triple, quintuple the number painted on the population sign. They stroll into town from the cemetery that overlooks the river, all the children who died young, Miss Goetz too, those great-aunts and great-uncles and their aged friends. They take up positions in the shops, on the sidewalk, in other people's parlours, and now I see my own dear mother, sitting at the piano beside an old man with a violin.

And I am everywhere among them, a toddler, a child too, a teenager skating round and round the arena to all the old songs, "Now and Then There's a Fool" and "Walk On By." I wander down the main street, eating vinegar-soaked potato chips from a bag split down the side, watching two-toned Ford Fairlanes cruise by. I wait outside the church door, beside the row of polished black cars, pulling at the scalloped edges of my short white gloves. And I sit at the kitchen table in my own house, watching my father walk quickly past the corner of our street, heading up the hill, though he comes to us eventually, and from the doorway mouths words that fix forever in my memory the keening of car brakes I've just heard.

I don't know how they bear it, the ones who never left. How they walk through streets so obstacled, past landscape that won't be still. But perhaps they learn to make allowances, to ignore the shifting architecture, find ways to make the ghosts stay in their place. Perhaps only those of us who try to leave and then come home are so undone.

This street? Oh, yes, it leads up the hill. But, really, I'd rather not. The village is not large, yet this walk always wears me out. I don't do it every time I visit, only once a year, when a certain chill is in the air. Or at odd times, like this, when it seems to soothe me to remember.

But I never go up there, past where the sidewalk ends, where the chalk boy lies, Karl's silhouette, traced in white on the grass.

2.

When the telephone rings, she picks it up quickly, as she has been instructed to do. She does not expect the call to be for her. This is the office line.

It will likely be a farmer telling her that a lamb is in trouble or a cow is down. She'll flick on the radio phone and repeat the veterinarian's call letters over and over until he hears her voice crackling from his truck radio as he walks across the barnyard, away from a birthing calf he has pulled out with a block and tackle or, worse, sawn into pieces and removed bit by bit. She might have to sit for hours, repeating the code dozens of times before he answers, but she'll persist.

The first night she babysat Karl, she hadn't understood most of what the farmers said in their uninflected tones. Tell the doc I've got a cow down, one had mumbled gruffly. Fallen down, down with the flu? Nothing in the turn of phrase had given her pause and so she'd simply added it to the list that she read aloud when, hours later, Karl's father returned. But he'd cut her short with his raging. Down meant half-dead; how stupid was she anyway? She'd probably caused a valuable animal to die. He'd beat the air with his fists and yelled words she'd never heard, coming as she did from a family where no voice was ever raised and no one cursed, no matter what.

She learned quickly after that. What it meant when a cow was down (milk fever, imminent death), the particulars of other diseases too: strangles and blackleg, greasy pig and sleepy foal sickness, moon blindness, the circling disease. At night, after Karl was in bed and her homework was done, she would arrange pillows embroidered with quetzals behind her on the couch and study the veterinary texts, repeating words aloud as if learning a foreign language: superficial sesamoidean ligament, papillomatosis, pyelonephritis. She marvelled at the exotic, significant sound of the official names of things, spavin, dystocia, urolithiasis, which the farmers with insistent matter-of-factness would call lameness, a hard birth, and water belly.

She especially liked the diagrams, the fine line drawings of nerve networks, blood pathways, organs, muscles, and bones, labelled with terms such as coffin joint, crypts of

Lieberkühn, and familiar words like chestnut that, forever after, would be overlaid with another meaning so that when she smelled red-brown nuts roasting on a street vendor's cart, she would see the horny knob on the inside of a horse's leg, feel a brightly coloured quetzal at her back.

Sometimes, if Karl's father got a call just as he was about to drive her home, he'd take her along to the farm. She has watched as he plunged his arm up to the shoulder inside the vaginal folds of a sheep, turning the lamb as the mother strained, easing it out at last and laying it, slimy and spindly-legged, on the straw, handing her a rag to rub it down while he tended to the ewe. And once, when he saw her eagerness, he took her hand and moved it over a heifer's right flank, showing her how to palpate the flesh until she felt the calf moving inside, teaching her the name of what she did: ballottement.

For four years, she has minded Karl after school and on evenings like tonight when his mother is out. A few times she has moved into their house for a week, minding him day and night while his parents visit Mexico, the place where his father grew up. Now that she is seventeen, she sometimes helps in the clinic too, passing instruments as Karl's father cuts out the wombs of cats, dispensing drugs to men who silently point to what they want for their sows' cracked teats and bloody scours, avoiding the names of intimate body parts, though the words hang indelicately in the air anyway, mixing with fresh manure from the farmers' boots and the vapour of dog and cat piss that seeps from the kennels in the back.

She picks up the telephone. It is not a farmer. The call is

for her. She recognizes the man's name. He is an editor at the local newspaper where she sends school news, but he is talking so quickly she can't make sense of what he is saying.

—You won't know them, I expect . . . much younger than you . . . need your help.

—Pardon? she says. —I don't understand.

—You haven't been listening to the radio?

—No.

—Geez.

He pauses so long she thinks he may have hung up, then he says, —Look . . . there's been an accident. Five kids from your school. And the mother of one of them. A train hit their car around suppertime. They were on their way home from football practice. No one got out alive. I figured you'd have heard.

—No.

—Listen, I'm sorry, but I need pictures of the boys. For the paper. I thought, since you're the editor of the yearbook, maybe you could get them for us. We need them first thing in the morning. We'll pay, of course.

—Sure. I guess so.

She struggles to think. —The janitor gets there at seven-thirty. Is that soon enough? But, who is it? Who's dead? I mean, I'll need their names.

They arrange to meet at eight the next morning by the front door of the school, then she hangs up and sits for a long time at the table, staring at the back of the envelope where she hastily scrawled the names. She finds a clean piece of paper and recopies each one neatly, arranging them in alphabetical order. When she's finished, she reads them off, pronouncing each name aloud. The wife of one of her favourite teachers. And his son. And the boy she'd argued with that afternoon at school, throwing his article at his feet, demanding a rewrite by morning or else. The editor was wrong. She knows them all. Knew them all, she corrects herself. They're dead.

Karl is calling from the bathroom. She leaves the table and goes to him. His sweater is wadded over his head, his arms caught in the folds of wool, exposing a smooth curve of belly, a nub of penis that bobs as he squirms.

— Don't look, he says.

— Hold still, silly. I'm not looking, for heaven's sake.

She pushes his elbows through the arm holes. His hands dart to cover his private parts. As she lifts off the sweater, she sees his face, his eyes crossed, tongue lolling.

— Aaarggghhhh, he says.

She starts to laugh, but the sound wobbles in her throat, shifts pitch peculiarly, and she pulls him to her, presses her forehead into his hair, hair that smells warm and sour, like a classroom filled with children, living, breathing children, and it ruins her.

— Hey! Cut it out! he whines, pushing her away.

She takes him by the shoulders, spins him around, and gives him a little shove. — Go on. Have your bath. You're eight years old. You can do it yourself. Call me when you're in bed. I'll come tuck you in.

Later, when he is safely asleep, she turns on the kitchen radio, keeping the volume low. As each station finishes its report, she tunes to another, the story endlessly repeating itself. The engineer spotting the car on the tracks, jamming on the brakes, unable to stop, the sickening impact. The worst car-train accident on record, the announcer says. The diesel engine of the train pushing the station wagon a mile down the tracks, sparks flying, the scream of steel on steel. The bodies inside looked like they'd been ripped apart, a witness sobs. Farmers, their wives, and children running across the fields, stumbling over freshly ploughed clods of earth, pulling on jackets against the cold, crying out to each other, trying not to look at the faces of the passengers pressed against the windows of the train, covering their mouths with their hands as if to contain what might escape, their eyes straining for a glimpse of wreckage, or worse.

Early the next morning, she backs her father's Buick out of the garage. The sun barely whitens the eastern sky as she turns north onto the river road. It is the Thursday before Thanksgiving. The weather has turned sharp. The river flows thick and brown, sluggish with the cold. Cornfields already turned for the winter lie black and exposed. Yellow lights glow in milkhouses and farm kitchens she drives past, but she doesn't notice. What she sees is the torpid river, the broken earth, and, in the kitchen gardens, shrivelled leaves, barren stalks, and here and there, a curve of pumpkin grey with hoarfrost.

The janitor is waiting for her. She'd called him the night before. He walks with her down echoing halls to the year-book room, waits as she fits her key in the lock.

—A shame, he says finally. —A real shame.

She closes the door on him. Pulling off her coat, she hurries to the file boxes of school pictures and flips through the names. When she finds the first photograph, she wipes one arm along the tabletop to make room, and when all five are set out, she spaces them precisely, like portraits in a gallery, like a row of disembodied heads. Did they do that, she wonders? Did they drag the bodies from the wreck and lay them out on the grass, side by side, straightening their limbs, gathering up the severed bits and setting them in place so that under the sheet or blanket these boys would seem whole again?

The five faces grin up at her, hair combed down in neat Beatle-bangs. Shy, reluctant smiles, cocky smirks. If only they had known, sitting in front of the photographer, bearing the taunts of the other boys, that they were composing their faces for the last time. Ready now, give us a smile, that's good, next. She fixes on the triangle of flesh at the open neck of one boy's shirt and, above it, his Adam's apple, fully exposed. Suddenly, she is overcome with embarrassment for them.

She expected to break down and cry. She thought that when eyes and lips and hair were fitted to the words of this disaster, she would be devastated by grief, but her calm only intensifies. She finds it curious. These faces look just the same this morning as they did yesterday. All that has changed is meaning. Then, they were pictures of the living. Now, they are portraits of the dead.

She labels each photograph, slides them into a large manila envelope, and carefully prints the name of the editor and the newspaper on the outside. Her senses have grown extraordinarily acute. She notices the arc of the pen's gold nib, the bubble of ink that accumulates at the end of each downward stroke, the delicately pebbled pattern in the floor tile as she walks back down the hall to the front entrance to wait for the editor.

—Thanks for this, he says, when he arrives a few minutes later. —I'll be in touch.

The halls are filling with students now. The sounds, usually boisterous, are muffled. When she walks past friends, she sees them as if from a great distance, watches as some girls weep and others lean against their lockers, eyes closed. Even the boys have abandoned bravado. Gone is the good-natured punching, the jostling, the leers.

The day passes. She feels oddly out of place, aware that what she did for the newspaper somehow implicates her in the catastrophe, prohibits her from sharing in the retelling, which goes on too long, she thinks. She leaves school early, taking the highway home, not the river road. She wants to see houses, children playing, other drivers in other cars. At a stop sign, though the highway is deserted, she lingers, her foot light on the brake.

If she turns left, she will come to a country road, and if she turns left again, she will see it, the place where the road meets the railway tracks, where the engineer grabbed the brake, where the boys turned, disbelieving, toward the on-coming train. Maybe if she saw it, the place where their lives came to an end, it would rouse her from this haze that has enveloped her like a premonition, a disturbing memory she can't quite recall, or the vestige of a dreadful dream.

Nothing strikes her as sufficient. The day is neither dull nor cold enough; her footsteps from the car to her house, inadequately ponderous and slow. But maybe, she thinks, that's how, in real life, one takes a tragedy to heart. Not with wild tears and gnashing of teeth, but quietly, with a sombre embrace.

She calls hello to her mother, who is ironing in the basement, then, vaguely hungry, she goes to the kitchen and makes herself a peanut-butter and honey sandwich and a cup of Ovaltine. The back door opens, followed by the sound of the newspaper hitting the floor. She picks up the paper and sits at the kitchen table. The pictures of the boys that she handed over to the editor this morning are lined up now above the fold. Below is a photograph of the mutilated vehicle.

The story fills half the newspaper. There are reports of the accident, interviews with family and friends, features on each of the dead, details of the funerals that will be held in a nearby town on Saturday. Shaped in words on a page, the event takes on substance, and she sighs with the terrible sadness of it. Now I know death, she thinks.

The sound of a car braking sharply interrupts her. A thin, high-pitched screech, like the scrape of fingernails on slate, cut short by a slap to the wrist. She looks out the window, wondering what could have happened, but all she sees is her father hurrying past, not turning at the corner, but continuing up the hill.

She returns to the newspaper and makes her way through each of the articles. It is almost dark when she hears the distinctive rasp of her father's shoes against the mat. It goes on for so long that she looks up from her reading. He is standing in the doorway of the kitchen. His skin is very white.

—Karl is dead, he says. —Hit by a car.

She is in her bedroom, in her rocking chair. Her fingers clutch the wooden arms. She rocks and she rocks. Faster and faster, she rocks. The blue wall is sky, she'll go over the top, like a swing. She rocks and rocks, faster and faster she swings, she rocks and rocks and rocks.

Her mother's hand covers hers. —Shhh, she says.

Karl's lips are not quite smiling. His shirt is white, the collar open at the neck. There is dirt under his fingernails.

—Doesn't he look natural, someone beside her says. —So peaceful, don't you think?

No, he never looked like that alive. He squirmed and twitched, even when he slept.

She wants to stand up and order the funeral organ un-plugged or a livelier tune played, the chairs folded away or, better yet, set in rows back to back for a game of musical chairs. Let's play make-believe, let's pretend, she'll say, and he'll sit up and cross his eyes and burst out laughing, Fooled you again!

Instead she watches, her fingertips so tight against her lips that she stops her own breath as the coffin lid is pulled down and bolted firmly shut. She hears the mournful songs, she mouths the prayers, and she waits beside the church door, pulling at her gloves while his family and their friends bend into long black cars. Between the rows of barren trees, she drives with her family to the cemetery just outside the village, where pallbearers lower the box with the little boy's body into the squared-off, smooth-edged hole. And she listens as shovelful after shovelful of earth hits the wood.

People are gathering at the house up the hill. The veterinarian and his wife have asked particularly that she come, there will be children to tend.

She walks past where the sidewalk ends, placing one foot carefully in front of the other, as she has learned to do. She thinks of nothing but moving forward and the fluted edge of the casserole dish that she clasps between her hands. She shuts her mind to trains, to cars, to a blue cowboy bedspread. She rehearses what she'll say when she knocks on the door. All the while, she looks steadfastly down, at the edge of the dish, at the ground.

And there he is: a silhouette in white, askew on the grass, legs bent, arm flung by his head, as if he's just rolled over, swept the leaf-fan aside.

She stops, stands transfixed. She cannot go on.

3.

The telephone rings. I walk to it, continuing the conversation with my new husband's parents, lifting the receiver expertly just before the answering machine clicks on.

—It's Mom, I hear my sister say. —She's had another coronary. You'd better come.

I've been expecting this call for ten years, since my mother had her first attack. Waited for it all my adult life, it seems. In my dreams, in the darkly polished niches of the night, in those hushed interstices in a conversation when, they say, an angel passes over, I reinforce my heart, thinking, This is the time. And yet, now that the call has finally come, it catches me unawares. My hand puts down the receiver and a succession of other hands, dreamt and imagined, hang up theirs too, one by one by one.

I don't return to the curious, eager faces around the dining table. Although I live as close to my parents' village as I ever have, it is still a four-hour drive away, too far to be summoned except in an emergency.

—It's my mother, I call as I run up the stairs. —I have to leave. Right now.

A suitcase. Underwear. Books to read in the waiting room. I've done this before. What else? Something black, a dress, in the event of a funeral. I take one out of the closet, then put it back. I will not imagine burials. Instead, in my memory, I search for my mother at her loveliest, in her teal-blue dress, yes, the one with the low scoop neck, flounced with crinolines, her ankles lovely in high heels, aquamarines flashing at her ears as she dances with my father through the living room, waiting to leave for the Mardi Gras dance. I hold this image, a quarantine against others, but believing, too, in the power of such thoughts.

My husband comes into the room and begins to throw his things into a suitcase.

−You don't have to come, I say. −Your parents are visiting. They've travelled so far. I can call and let you know if something happens.

−My parents will be fine. They'll stay the night and lock up when they leave in the morning. It's already arranged.

He takes my shoulders and turns me to him. − I'm not letting you go alone. Do you understand? I want to be with you.

I lean against his chest. There's so much I haven't told this man.

−I love you, I whisper.

Within ten minutes we are in the car, heading west. It is just after eight. With luck, we can be there by midnight.

I sit rigid, staring out the window into the darkness, not seeing the landscape reel by. Pain, I know, carves a trajectory so indelible that long after a wound heals, any recurrence, however minor, can send a spasm of undiminished intensity along the original path. And so, although I don't know yet how serious my mother's condition is, my heart is racing, the muscles in my stomach clench. My body feels this journey to her bedside as if it were the first.

That other time it was morning, and my oldest son sat beside me. He was fourteen. His father and younger brother were in Europe, their trip a gift from me. I'd done the same for this son when he was ten. That was the age at which I'd travelled as a child, and I wanted to give my children what I'd been given: a legacy of place and memory.

None of the family was in the hospital room when my son and I arrived. The nurse said, – Go on in, but just for a few minutes.

And so we did, unprepared, my son entering through the door I held open, not knowing what he'd see, her skin so waxen, her eyes pressed closed as if for the last time. The only signs of life were the machines that hummed around her, the drip of fluids through the body that lay on the bed.

I went to her and kissed her cheek. Out of the corner of my eye, I saw my son backing away from his first glimpse of how life wanes. I caught him in my arms, this quiet boy who loves music, who finds eloquence not in words but in the interplay of silence and sound, my first-born son, named for a child I knew who had died. In the year my son was eight, I'd watched him anxiously, especially as the leaves turned red. I'd tortured myself with the thought that, in giving him a dead child's name, I'd laid a curse on him. It wasn't so, of course, and for once I'd felt grateful for life's stubborn randomness.

My three sisters and my father were in the waiting room. The doctors allowed my mother only one visitor at a time, five minutes every hour. None of us left the hospital. We fetched tea and sandwiches, read and dozed, alert always for those few moments when the one whose turn it was to see her would come back and report to the rest of us.

I think she heard me, her eyes flickered a little, a sister would say, each wanting to be the one who was there when she first awoke.

I told her we're all praying for her, said another, and the others nodded and murmured that they had said the same.

Then they knelt on the cold linoleum and asked God to do His will.

I was younger then, more self-indulgent: I refused to bow my head. Instead I went to the public telephone and tried again to reach my husband, leaving messages at hotels, at the homes of relatives, even embassies, in half a dozen European countries, giving precise instructions as to where I could be reached and how.

When it was my turn to hold my mother's hand, I said quietly, —You can go if you want to. We'll be fine.

But even behind those waxen eyelids, she knew that I was lying. She could always tell.

Then, I could not bear for her to die. I could not imagine being even more alone. Can I bear it now?

I breathe into the darkness, Please, please don't die. But the truth is, I don't want to make her stay. I know from what she's said to me that she is tired, she's ready to go.

I reach across to the man who is my husband now and rest my hand on his. In ten years so much, everything, has changed.

You can leave, I'll be fine, I whisper soundlessly to the night. And this time, I realize, I mean it.

I don't see any of my family when my husband and I arrive at the hospital. I press the buzzer outside the heavy, wired-glass door of cardiac intensive care.

—I've come to see my mother.

—And what's her name?

I feel my husband's hand on my arm. I glance over my

shoulder, and there they are, framed at the end of the hall, my father and my sisters. I turn back to the nurse who is telling me, —I'm sorry. She died just ten minutes ago. Would you like to see her?

And so we go in. Her skin is very white, but her cheek, when I touch my fingertips to it, is warm, though the flesh is already collapsing against bone, her lips drawing back from her teeth, this gentle loving woman, defiant only in death.

In the chill of the morning, I walk with my husband through the village, finding a certain solace in remembering, although I avoid the street that goes up the hill and the white outline on the grass I remember there. I see it anyway. One death recalls every other.

In the afternoon, my sisters and I gather our mother's clothes and the jewellery she will wear, and go with my father to choose the coffin for her body. Later, we stand for hours beside her in the windowless room ripe with flowers that have no scent. Lined up according to age, we shake hands with the villagers who slow-step past. Our husbands are with us too, though the children we release from obligation, for this body dressed in a tailored blue suit and pearl-and-diamond earrings is too much for them, even now that her cheeks are rouged and powdered and her lips are drawn together in a tight, distracted smile.

At the house, we go through her things. In her purse, by her bed, in her dresser drawers, we find scraps of paper, scribbled messages to herself, a record of her decline, her dwindling capabilities. This woman who never complained, who always put others first, acutely known only to herself.

In her absence, we become her. Politely, we divide up the topazes, aquamarines, and pearls, each of us urging the finer things on the others. As we sort her daintily embroidered blouses and A-line skirts into piles, some to give away, some to throw out, we find ourselves saying what she would have said: Well, look on the bright side, and, There but for the grace of God go I. We deliberately find excuses to repeat her words of wisdom. To the sister who brings a tea tray to the little bedroom strewn with nightgowns, photographs, and books, we say, That's another star in your crown. And, Pride goeth before a fall, we say in unison to the sister who preens a little at a compliment, to which she replies, If you can't say anything nice, don't say anything at all. Then, finally, the best one of all: Everything will be all right when you have a man. And we laugh until we cry, loving her goodness, resolving to spare our children this litany that echoes in our lives, knowing, even as we make our brave promises, that we've perfected one of our own already, and that our children will forswear it, too.

We never speak of her as if she's here, for she is not. None of us can sense our mother in these rooms. As each of my three sisters recalls a woman not quite like the one I know, it occurs to me that she has not left us altogether, but has passed into an antechamber, one walled with mirrors, where her image reflects four ways, one for each of us who holds her dear.

In the days between her death and her burial, the telephone is rarely silent. When I answer it late one night, my heart contracts, for it is the voice of my first husband.

—I want to come pay my respects, he says.

I purse my lips, force back the impulse to give with both hands, which is still, as always, my first response to someone's need. I think of my sons, knowing this man's part in them, and I think of my new husband, who gives me so much, weighing his rights and theirs. And I think of myself, too, admitting that I do not want him here, that he has no place among us now, recognizing this as ungenerous, unchristian, knowing it is in some part retribution for his refusal to include me when his own father, a man I loved, died. For these reasons, and others I no longer feel obliged to explain, I say, —No. You'll have to find some other way to grieve.

I do not wear black to speak the eulogy. I'll wear red to your funeral, I'd always joked, but I don't. I find a simple suit in muted damask that I think she might have liked instead.

The words I speak are not mine alone. We've made them together, my sisters, my father, and I. When I finish, I touch the polished surface of the casket where she lies and return to my seat behind the others. My oldest son puts his arm around me, my younger son takes my hand in his, and I sit down between them as my husband leans close to stroke my hair. I sink into their love as if I've just come home.

My husband drives my father's car in the funeral procession. It's the first time I've seen my father sitting in the passenger seat since he had a driver in Brazil. Sometimes my mother kept the Buick and collected him at the factory after work, but she'd always slip across the seat as soon as he appeared, giving up the wheel before he asked. I study him from the back seat now, where I sit with my sons. His posture is as firm as ever, but as he looks out the window, his face turned to me in profile, I see his features sag as if in disbelief and disappointment at finding his landscape so entirely changed.

The cemetery is crowded with my mother's mourners, weeping quietly by her grave, not for her so much as for our loss. Each of the family takes a solitary pink rose from the bouquet that blankets the coffin lid. I hold mine to my breast and look across the rows of headstones.

Phantoms are clustering at every tomb, graves folding open as the dear departed rise to grieve each other's ghosts. Only one small grave stays closed. I hear the echo of earth against wood, and I realize, then, that every pain must at last be felt.

4.

Come, little child, open your grave, too.

If you'd been born in Mexico, in the country of your father, if that was where you'd died, you'd be an angel now; you'd have been one all these years. They'd have laid you out in green satin stitched with golden stars, slipped foil sandals on your feet, a crown of flowers in your hair, and, over that sweet, silly face of yours, draped a handkerchief of silk, for worms never touch flesh draped in silk.

I'd have danced at your funeral then, sung with music-makers, spirit-drunk, and cheered as rockets burst the sky. I'd have brought *milagros*, silver eyes and lips and hearts, for the hem of the Virgin's gown, prayed for miracles that I myself might perform.

If only I had known you there, where life ends as it begins, with tears of love, and laughter too. Where grief, it's understood, causes injury, especially to the dead, for a child buried in sorrow suffers sorrow through eternity, and it was I, holding fast to my misery, who ensured our pain.

Come back with me to the village, Karl, to the grassy side of the road. We'll gather up the ghosts, my mother too, and with the brightest leaves of autumn trailing in our hair we'll dance you to the churchyard, lay you finally to rest.

And every year, when the air turns cold, I'll light fireworks on your grave. I'll set candles flickering on the headstone and sing you merry songs as the wax, white and fragrant as frangipani, slides down the chiselled grooves over-laying, at last, that dusty silhouette and raising high the words, IN LOVING MEMORY.

ACKNOWLEDGEMENTS

Some of these stories have been previously published, often in substantially different form: "The Still Point" in *Saturday Night Magazine* (March, 1993); "Taken for Delirium" in *Treasures of the Place: Three Centuries of Canadian Nature Writing* (Douglas & McIntyre, 1995), and in *Living in Harmony: Nature Writing by Women in Canada* (Orca Book Publishers, 1996); and the first section of "The Day of the Dead" in *Writing Home: A PEN Canada Anthology* (McClelland & Stewart, 1997).

The passage quoted on page 154 is from *Mother's Remedies* by Dr. T. J. Ritter, published by G.H. Foote Pub. Co., Detroit, Michigan, 1910. And the couplet on page 183 was found quoted in the introduction to the 1939 edition of Graham Greene's travel book, *The Lawless Roads*. Every effort has been made to locate the song "Off to the Beach," quoted on page 54. It may be a figment of the author's imagination, or a private family ritual, but if not, she would be pleased to hear from the lyricist or the song's publisher. The first epigraph on page vii is taken from "Window on Memory (II)" from *Walking Words* by Eduardo Galeano, translated by Mark Fried. Copyright © 1993 by Eduardo Galeano. Translation copyright © 1995 by Mark Fried. Reprinted by permission of the author and W.W. Norton & Company, Inc.

The second epigraph is taken from *Light in August* by William Faulkner. Copyright © 1932, 1959, published by Vintage International in 1990 and reprinted by permission of Random House, Inc. The song lyric on page 75 is from "Daydream," words and music by John Sebastian. Copyright © 1966 (renewed 1994) by Alley Music Corp. and Trio Music Co., Inc. All rights in Canada controlled and administered by Beechwood Music Corp. All rights reserved. International copyright secured. Used by permission. The excerpt on page 135 is from the poem "The Third One" by Yannis Ritsos, translated from the Greek by Nikos Stangos and published in *Gestures and Other Poems 1968-70*, Cape Goliard Press, London, 1971. Copyright © 1971 by Yannis Ritsos. Translation copyright © 1971 by Nikos Stangos. Reprinted by permission of publishers Jonathan Cape.

—◠◠—

I am grateful for the financial assistance of the Canada Council for the Arts and the Ontario Arts Council, both the Writers' Reserve and Works-in-Progress programs. These grants were instrumental in the successful completion of this work.

For her generous support, both professional and personal, I thank my agent, Bella Pomer; for their skilled assistance, Lisan Jutras and Anita Chong; for valuable discussions along the way, Pam Benson, Matt Cohen, Pam Green and Reg Martin, Genni Gunn, Norman Levine, Connie Rooke, Carolyn Smart, Dianna Symonds, Ellen Stafford, Phyllis

Amber and Sydney Weisbord, and Merrily Weisbord; for assistance with translations, Eudora Potter, Gloria B. Díaz, and Doug Babbington; for sharing their own versions of these stories with me, my friends Joan Jenner, Faith Baldwin, and Sharon Wright, and my large and generous family, including my sisters, Joey, Donna, and Ginny, my sons, Karl and Erik, my first husband and his mother and father, my Aunt Marion and Uncle David, all the men and women of my grand-mother's generation who took me under their wing, and, especially, my father and my mother. I miss her every day.

Finally, my heartfelt thanks to my editor, Ellen Seligman, for her enthusiasm, her keen insight, and gentle insistence; and to my companion on this journey and all others, Wayne Grady, as always, my deepest gratitude and love.

Bernard Clark

Merilyn Simonds was born in Winnipeg, Manitoba, and spent her childhood in Brazil. Her previous book, *The Convict Lover* (1996), was shortlisted for the Governor General's Award, the Arthur Ellis Award, and was named one of the best books of 1996 by *Quill & Quire*, the *Globe and Mail*, *Elm Street*, and *Maclean's*. *The Convict Lover* premiered as a stage play at Toronto's Theatre Passe Muraille in 1998.

Simonds has worked as a freelance writer and a magazine editor, has taught courses in literary non-fiction, and has been a guest lecturer at colleges and universities in the U.S. and Canada. She has won several national awards for her magazine writing.

She lives outside Kingston, Ontario, with her husband, writer and translator Wayne Grady. She is at work on a novel.